Love In Between

The White Lines ©

C. Wilson

D1621921

<u>DEDICATION</u>

This re-release is for all my loyal readers that read the first version. FORGET everything that you think you know. This is a new Ty and Toya. To my new readers get ready for the roller coaster love ride that you are about to get on. Enjoy,

C. Wilson

"I'm gone start this shit off by talking straight facts. Without me, none of this shit would have ever been birthed! I paved the way for the Bushwick hustlers y'all know today. From *Truth is Stranger than Fiction* y'all know T.S.S. but my squad are the niggahs who started it all. Like, I don't think y'all understand how me and my team used to give it up back in the day. My life didn't really do a 360 until I met my shorty though. Shit was crazy back then, shit was—huh? I can't tell the story myself? Alright, whatever man. C. Wilson is hounding me y'all so let me shut up and let her tell the story for me. Keep up aight?"

C. Wilson

"School Days"

Brooklyn 2006

Chapter 1

The beginning

"Psst... Yo, Ma can I talk to you?"

"Yoooo, come here sweetie."

"Gorgeous. Can I get your number?"

Toya ignored the random men that called to her as she traveled through the streets of Flatbush towards school. She knew better than to stop and talk to anyone. Growing up, Toya's mother, Kinsey, taught her daughter all the pros and cons of becoming a woman. Answering a catcall from a random guy in the street was forbidden. If a man wanted to approach her, he had to do so correctly.

For Toya, a guy expressing their admiration towards her in the street was an everyday thing. At the tender age of seventeen she was fully morphed into her womanly figure. Her perky breasts were nice, firm, well-rounded C-cups, her stomach was flat as a board, and her shapely hips, ass and thighs filled any jeans she wore to capacity. Not to mention her nice mahogany complexion, green-colored, doe-like eyes and layered, mid-back length silky hair complimented her high, sleek cheekbones. Toya's beauty was rare, and she damn sure knew it. Compared to other girls around her way, she knew she was the shit.

$$$

"You are late young lady," Ms. Thompson said with a stern voice as she watched her late student slowly drag her feet into the classroom. She spoke loudly to make sure that everyone in the class had heard her. All of Latoya's classmates looked up. Some greeted her with smiles and waves.

"Hey Toya," one boy said louder than the others.

"Hey Qua," she cooed as she walked model-like to her seat.

Watching the interactions between the two, a table filled with girls just sucked their teeth and rolled their eyes. *There go them hating ass bitches,* she thought.

She couldn't be too mad at them because they had a lot to hate on. She came to school every day laced in the hottest shit, she had a fresh wash and set every week and all the niggas in the twelfth grade broke their necks to speak to her; it didn't matter if they had a girl or not.

"Stop being so uptight Ms. T, it's my last day of school," she shot back in a *get off my back* manner.

Today, she wasn't going to let anything get under her skin. She was a senior with more than enough credits, her test scores were superb, and her grade point average was a 4.0. Her future was looking promising. The next day was supposed to be hers to own. She was finally going to be eighteen. Midnight meant so much to her because at twelve on the dot, she would be a woman. At twelve on the dot, she was finally going to let Ty rob her of her v card.

She was nervous, ecstatic and curious all at the same time. She had already discussed with her mother the night prior how after school she would be staying the night at her best friend, Leah's, house.

Leah knew Toya's real intentions of staying the night with Ty, but she promised to stick to the little plan that they had formed. If anyone was to call Leah's house phone and ask to speak to Toya, she would stall until she could make a three-way call to Toya's phone. Putting her on the line as if she had just simply passed her the phone. The plan was perfect. It was nothing new to them; on several occasions like tonight they did the same thing.

The 2:15 bell rang out loudly through the halls. This was what she waited for, the end of the school day. As Toya left school, she told Leah that she would keep texting her to check in. They hugged and then bid farewells. Leah watched her friend walk away towards the train. She randomly caught this huge feeling of butterflies in the pit of her stomach.

She had a terrible sentiment that something bad was going to happen, she just didn't know what it was.

$$$

Toya sat comfortably on the J train as she scrolled through her call log until she came across the name, *Ty Baby*. She listened intently as ringing filled her ears.

"Yo," a husky voice said coolly through the receiver.

"Hey Boo, I'm on my way," she said sexily.

Toya tried to sound as seductive as possible as she whispered through the phone erotically. On the other line Ty began to become aroused; he had an itch that only Toya could scratch for two years now and he couldn't wait to crack her shell. He knew he could, and he knew that tonight would be that special night.

"Aight Ma, don't keep me waiting," he said with a boyish grin before he hung up.

$$$

Ty breathed deeply as he rested comfortably on top of his king-sized bed. His folded arms stood strong behind his head. He loved spending time alone; that was when he let his mind roam free. Breaking from his thoughts, he looked around and realized that he had a lot of cleaning to do.

Ty was twenty, hood raised and proud of it. At the tender age of sixteen he got out in the streets and rubbed elbows with big time hustlers who had been in the game for years. By the age of seventeen his feet were wet in the game. He was just now starting out, but he had a lot to prove to other infamous New York hustlers that were already well known and well respected. Over the course of four years, he bullied his way into the elite's round table and established himself in the streets as *Ty the Gunner*.

If Ty wanted it, Ty took it, and any nigga dumb enough to cross him knew exactly what was to come, death. He was ruthless in the streets and held no remorse, but with Toya, his whole demeanor changed; it was more soft, relaxed and level headed. He didn't know what this girl possessed that kept him so calm, but he knew that he was addicted to her. As he lay comfortably, a huge grin spread wide across his face, showing off his deep dimples. He still remembered the very first time he had ever laid eyes on Toya...

The sun was high, and the sky and the sticky, humid July air was flooded with roaring engines and blasting stereo systems. Bushwick's block parties brought out the finest hustlers and the even finer bitches. Love at first sight seemed way too farfetched for Ty, but it was something about this girl that baffled him when she came strolling down his block.

She walked confidently with a Spanish girl at her side. Her sloppy bun bounced with each strong stride she took.

"Yo bro, I know you see that sexy ass jump off over there with the big ass wag," Bleek said to Ty as he sat on the stoop comfortably with his older brother. He nodded his head in the direction of the two girls.

"You better be talking about the Spanish broad," Ty said with a smirk, although his eyes were dead serious.

Bleek, sensing that his right hand had his eye on his choice, he replied, "Well, then I'll settle for the Spanish Mamí. Do you bro."

Both men sipped Grey Goose straight, no chaser, from their Styrofoam ice cups. They already had their eyes on their marks, now their next move was how to attack.

Present day...

Once Ty made his move there was no coming back from it. He remembered seeing her and wanting her. Always getting what he wanted, rightfully, she was now his. As time progressed Toya learned to love his demanding presence. When he stepped onto a scene, he held the attention of everyone. She was amazed at how he could intimidate the most thorough of a group of gangster men.

His voice was strong, and he always held his composure. The way he conducted himself drove her crazy. At first, they weren't exclusive. Ty was skeptical because he was eighteen and she was just only sixteen. Two years had passed and on an intellectual level Ty saw that Toya was well beyond her years. A friendship was their foundation and a deep love was what blossomed.

Ty hopped out of the bed and went straight towards the living room to look for the television remote. Once he found it, he turned to channel 850, the R&B station.

It's me and you now,
I've been waiting.

I think I'm gonna make that move now.
Baby tell me if you like it.

The vocals of Cassie bumped through the surround sound. Ty shook his head, completely annoyed. *Dumb ass song,* he thought, but he left the station knowing that Toya liked to listen to music like that. He began to do a little bit of straightening up. His Nike slippers hugged the plush, eggshell carpet as he walked towards his mother's room. Closing her door, he was grateful that she was away on one of her many "business trips," a ploy she had over the years to run off and get high.

Ty was no stranger to his mother's addiction to crack. He noticed when his own work began to come up short. Instead of chastising him at such a young age for selling an illegal substance, Ms. Diane just took from her son's stash here and there, praying that he didn't notice. But he did, and every once in a blue moon she went on huge binges taking half of her son's stash with her while in return leaving behind a note that contained the same exact words every time.

> *Something came up and I had to go handle*
> *business.*
> *I'll be back in a few days*
> *Love you,*
> *-Mommy xoxo*

It hurt Ty's heart to the core because he knew that with his temper, his line of work and his mother's addiction, that one day he would be pushed to harm her if he didn't create space between the two of them. He was due to move out in a month's time. But he had plans on still paying all her bills so that whenever she came home from her journeys, she would have somewhere to rest her head without the constant worry of turn off or eviction notices. Being that this trip was the longest she had taken, he had scoured the streets for her. After coming up empty he hoped that she wasn't dead in a ditch somewhere.

He couldn't come to terms with getting rid of his mother's apartment. This was the same apartment that he grew up in. His father, before his demise, was one of the biggest drug lords that the tri-state area had ever seen. He made sure that his family was well taken care of before he died. Unfortunately, the money that he left behind didn't even last a year; everyone was in a drought.

In total, Ty had seven sisters, all with different women, luckily for him he was the only boy. When he heard of his father's death, the day was a sweet and sour one for him. It just so happened that being as polygamist as his father was, that was his downfall. They say it's all fun and games until you're fucking someone else's wife. Sadly, Tyshawn Senior had to learn the hard way. He was shot point blank range in his back while on top of the neighbor's wife.

Ty had mixed feelings towards his old man; yes, he loved his father, but he hated the lifestyle that he lived. Everything crumbled for him the day he and his mother attended his father's funeral. All love he had for his old man quickly faded. While in attendance, an unfamiliar woman with five children beside her stood at the podium to the left of the closed, flowered casket.

All their faces had grief written all over. All twelve eyes gazed at the black and gold casket, stuck. Everyone silently in their head replayed memories of their own that they once shared with the dressed corpse. Everyone in the crowd sat quietly waiting for their whimpers to subside so that someone could speak. After moments of silence the woman standing lead gathered up enough courage to introduce herself as his father's wife.

Ty was pissed and confused all at the same time. Being just thirteen, he couldn't understand how his father could treat him so good but ignore his other children. He had his father's full name, his father lived with him and his mother and he had never, ever seen or heard of his other families. His father had other children, but Ty was his first and only boy; he was the baby. He took pride and drew close to his son.

The smell in the air always made him reminisce of happier times when his family was a family, when they were whole. He kept telling himself that things would get better. Deep down inside, he hoped that his mother would one day get right, and he wanted to be there to witness it but *once a fein, always a fein.* Snapping out of his inner thoughts, Ty sat on the couch and turned on his Xbox 360. He played his favorite game, Madden '06, until Toya arrived.

Chapter 2

Damn, I know I'm not nervous, Toya thought to herself as she walked up the stairs to Ty's building. She rang the bell labeled *Barnett* and then sat on the banister to wait for a response.

"I know that better be my baby girl," a playful, husky voice sang through the buzzer's intercom.

Toya blushed. "Yea, it's me," she responded.

She then heard a buzzing sound and was allowed access into the lavish brownstone building.

As she walked up the two flights of stairs to Ty's crib, her nervous feeling left her body. She made it up in her mind that she would be sexy for her man. She didn't want to seem like this inexperienced little girl, although she was. Her intentions were to shock the hell out of Ty. She was going to be on her grown woman shit. *Who runs from a thrill? Not*

Latoya Greene! she thought as she skipped the stairs by two.

She felt like she had a lot to prove knowing that Ty had several women in the past who were older and more experienced than she was. Little did she know, he had never loved anyone how he loved her. Just as she was about to knock on his front door, it swung open.

"Wussup Ma?" he said as he stood to the side, allowing her room to walk in.

Toya stood frozen. She looked at her man and was taken back when she realized just how sexy he was. She looked him up and down, took a deep breath and then overlooked him again. She was mesmerized by his nice, clean cut. His hair always looked curly when it was grown out but silky when it was cut down real low.

His twenty-five percent Spanish background showed in most of his features. The waves on top of his head would make a woman sea sick if she stared for too long. He wore a white wife beater that revealed his large chest tattoo written in script bold letters that read: *Only God Can Judge Me. God please don't judge me after tonight,* Toya thought as she licked her lips hungrily when she eyed his muscles. You could tell that he kept up with his physical features. It was obvious that he worked out a bit. Both his arms were toned and succulent.

The tattoos that covered his arms were neat and vibrant. All the artwork on his body could have been the work of Michelangelo. His nice, tanned, caramel skin was smooth and held no blemishes. This went perfect with those muscular features that Toya loved so much. His red and black Nike slippers matched his Nike basketball shorts.

Standing at six feet tall, his tall, muscular frame towered over Toya's five-foot-four-inch stature. She was Barbie doll sized and made especially for him.

"So, are you gonna come in or not?" he asked in his sexiest voice as he licked his full lips and smiled, showing his dimples that Toya was infatuated with.

"Yeah, I am," she said strongly.

Toya brushed past him putting on her sexiest strut. She sported a pair of athletic booty shorts with the letters *N I K E* plastered over the ass, a white v-neck tee and a pair of hot pink and white Air Max to match her shorts. Her overnight bag swung from her shoulder as she bounced across the hallway hardwood floors and onto the living room's nice plush carpet.

Ty watched as she walked over towards the couch and sat. Her walk was so hypnotizing. Patting the spot beside her, she motioned for him to sit.

Ring, Ring, Ring

Toya fumbled for her Nextel phone in a panic. She silently prayed that the call wasn't her mother. She looked at the cover of her phone and saw the name *Leah* sliding across the screen.

"Hello," she said, answering the phone in an unsure tone, not knowing if her mother would be on the other end or her homegirl.

"Hey girl, don't sound so scary, punk ass." Leah laughed through the phone.

"Shut up!" Toya said playfully as she continued, "Wussup girl?"

"I was just calling to see if you made it there safe. I had a bad feeling," Leah said worriedly.

"Aw, now who's the punk ass?" Toya chuckled as she continued, "Girl, I'm good."

"Okay cool, tell Tyshawn I said heyyyyy," Leah blurted through the phone loud enough for Ty to hear.

Ty tried his best to hide his annoyance as Toya spoke on the phone. He knew bitches like Leah a thousand miles away, a straight bird, a chicken head, a pigeon type of broad. Everything about her Ty didn't like, down to her cat-shaped eyes that looked so sneaky to him. He knew Leah was bad news for Toya the very first day that he had met her. He hoped that Toya would see what he did.

"Sorry baby," Toya said as she hung up the phone. "Now, where were we?"

The sexual grin she wore on her face made Ty slowly grow in his basketball shorts. He smiled as he walked over to her and leaned in for a kiss. As their tongues danced in each other's mouths, Ty pulled back.

"You ready to go?" he asked as he pulled at his shorts, situating its former position to hide the imprint that his semi-erect penis formed in them.

Confused, Toya asked, "Go where?"

Ty smiled showing his dimples. "We going out to eat. I'm thinking seafood."

Ty took a quick shower and stood in his closet with just a towel wrapped around his waist. Water beads dripped down his thick chest as he thought deeply. *What to wear? What to wear?* His eyes scanned over all his designer gear. He put on a white v-neck tee, his gray and white Jordan sweats to match his gray, white and baby blue Air Jordan XII.

After Toya took a quick shower, she switched into her light pink Juicy Couture Capri sweats, a white wife beater, and she put on her same pink and white Nikes. Once she grabbed her light pink Juicy Couture clutch, she was ready to go.

"Damn Ma, how much clothes you got in that little bag?" Ty joked.

"Trust me, I have way more that will shock you, but you'll see that later." She smirked.

Making sure that he had his wallet and house keys in his pocket, Ty signaled that it was time to go.

$$$

Ty and Toya walked outside hand in hand. He kissed her hand gently and then opened the passenger side car door for her. Once rested on top of the soft, cream leather interior Toya daydreamt about how fortunate she was to have a man like Ty. He was older, more experienced, had his own money, his own luxury foreign car, and his own crib, because his mother was hardly ever home. To top it off, he was one hundred percent faithful to her; Toya felt lucky.

Plugging his phone up to his car to listen to his own music instead of the radio, Ty began to rap hard, bopping his head to the beat.

I don't love 'em, I fuck 'em
I don't chase 'em, I duck 'em
I replace 'em with another one
You had to see she keep calling me BIG and
my name is Jay-Z
She be all on my dick, gradually

"Uh, this is my shit!" he yelled as he rapped some more and bopped his head even harder.

The trip to the restaurant felt like forever but once the sign read *Sammy's Fish box*, Toya was excited. She had told Ty that her aunt used to take her there all the time when she was younger. Ty tossed his keys to the valet as they walked into the restaurant.

Over the next three hours, they dug into their crab and lobster feast as they told jokes. They held deep conversations and reminisced about how they had first met.

"All I'm saying is, you were on a nigga and Leah's ass was definitely on Bleek. Don't trip baby girl we knew, well I definitely knew that I was the shit at that block party."

Ty spoke while chewed up crabmeat and rice circled around in his mouth. Toya hated his poor table manners, but that was something about Ty that just wasn't going to change. He continued talking, using his hands to get his point across.

"I saw some little niggas tryna holla at you, but I wasn't gonna cock block, I let 'em rock. It seemed to me like you could smell bullshit from miles away and Ma, I'm all about the real. Once I approached ya I saw in your eyes that you wanted a real niggah."

He took a sip of his Pepsi, burped and then continued.

"You wanted me shorty. Don't feel ashamed you were open. I tend to have that effect on bitches. I mean women."

Ty widened his eyes to jokingly show Toya just how open she was when they first met. Toya laughed so hard that tears came to her eyes. As she took a minute to reminisce, she could recall that it was Ty who was sweating her while she gave him no play. Just as she was about to respond to correct his ass, there was an interruption…

Ring, Ring, Ring!

Toya reached into her clutch and pulled out her cell phone. It read: *Leah.*

"Hello?" she answered nervously.

"LA FUCKING TOYA! I haven't spoken to your ass in almost eight hours!" Kinsey screamed through the phone at her daughter, frustrated at her disappearance.

"I know Ma, I'm sorry, me and Leah was getting stuff together for graduation. The time slipped my mind. In a few we're gonna go to your favorite spot, *Sammy's*. I could save you some food if you want."

Toya put on her baby voice hoping her mother would let her slide on this one. Kinsey couldn't help it. The sound of her only child giving her the baby voice softened her like butter, and she only went soft for two people in the world, her lover Lance and her daughter.

"Okay, that's fine. Well I don't want to be a party pooper miss birthday girl. Tell Leah I said enjoy y'all outing. I'll text or call you at twelve to say happy birthday if I'm up. I love you."

Right when Toya was about to respond to her mother, she heard a drunken, deep voiced rage in the background.

"Her hot in the pants ass ain't grown. She needs to get her ass here A.S.A.P!"

Toya could tell that her stepfather, Lance, was drunk by the way he slurred his words. Kinsey removed the phone from her mouth as she yelled.

"Shut the fuck up Lance! I said she can stay out tonight so that's that!"

A loud commotion erupted in Toya's ear and then her mother's line disconnected.

"I love you too, Ma."

Toya's voice was depressed and distant as she spoke to the dead line. Leah remained on the phone to make sure that her best friend was okay.

"I'm good Leah," she reassured and then hung up the phone. She was clearly annoyed. To Toya, all of this was regular. When Lance drank, he got violent and Kinsey was his personal punching bag. He never physically abused Toya but the way he watched her made her feel uneasy.

For the past seven years, Toya watched her mother get her ass beat time and time again. She used to look at her mother as strong, angelic and powerful, but ass whooping after ass whooping turned the woman Toya used to know into an angry, scorned beast that no one understood. Instead of taking her rage out on her attacker, Kinsey, took her rage out on everyone else.

"They're fighting again, huh?"

Ty held deep concern in his eyes as he looked at the saddened girl that sat across the table from him.

"Yea, it's nothing though." Toya brushed it off quickly as she tried her best to keep her emotions in check.

"Yo Ma, if you want me to, I will handle—" Toya cut him off by leaning over the table; she started kissing him gently. She didn't want to involve him in any of her problems at home.

The check came and Ty snatched it up once it hit the table. He parted with three bills and then placed the money onto the table. He motioned that it was time to go by reaching out his hand.

"You ready to go home?" he asked.

How lovely it would be for home to mean their home where she could go and stay. She would have no worries.

She wouldn't have to be bothered with her mother and stepfather's bullshit, a place where she could be happy, a place she could call home. The small, two-bedroom apartment in Flatbush with her mother and stepfather attacking each other every day was not home. Unbeknownst to Toya, Ty had intentions on moving her in with him to his new place next month.

He had too much respect for her to move her into his current home, another woman's throne. If he was going to live with the woman he loved, he had to make sure that she was the only lioness in the tribe. There was no way he would bring his lady into his mother's home. Ty envisioned it all. He saw Toya decorating the new condo that he had just purchased in Downtown Brooklyn. He knew that once he shared the news of her moving in with him, she would go interior decorator crazy. He couldn't wait;

he wanted the best for his lady, and he knew staying with him was just that.

Chapter 3

The drive back to Ty's house seemed longer than the drive out to the restaurant. Five minutes away from their destination a police cruiser with red, white and blue flashing lights pulled up directly behind them.

Whoop, Whoop!

Ty pulled over and cut his engine. He was too used to the protocol of what to do while getting pulled over, for it was far from new to him. Toya stiffened in her chair. She prayed that Ty didn't have any drugs on him or in his car. He quickly sensed her tension.

"Ma, I'm smarter than that, trust me, we good," he assured as he grabbed her thigh giving it a gentle squeeze to calm her.

Two clean uniformed officers pulled up to the vehicle; they both had flashlights in their hands to look through the tints of the windows. The officer on Ty's side of the car was an older black man with salt and pepper colored hair.

"Good evening young man. Do you know why we stopped you tonight?" he asked powerfully.

"I'm not too sure but enlighten me sir." Ty put on his most innocent voice.

"Well—"

The cop on Toya's side of the car cut the other officer off.

"One of your tail lights is out. Do you mind giving my partner your license and registration?"

The Spanish officer seemed antsy. He seemed like the type to judge niggas like Ty. You know, the kind of cop that took power and authority to the head.

Ty looked over and looked at his nameplate before he made a move. It read: *F. Vasquez. They're so full of shit!* he thought as his nose flared. He pulled himself together; the last thing that he wanted was to accidentally stir any problems.

"No problem sir," he said calmly and then began to reach into his dashboard to take out his registration.

"Here you go sir," Ty said confidently as he passed over his merchandise. He knew these cops had nothing on him. His insurance and license were good.

The two officers retreated into their vehicle leaving the couple alone for a moment.

"I really wish they would hurry the fuck up!" Toya was growing impatient.

"Yo Ma, chill out! They're coming right now."

The black cop handed Ty his license and registration.

"Ok Mr. Barnett, I'll let you and your lady friend off with a warning."

As Ty started the car and then peeled off, the Spanish cop yelled out, "Nice car!"

He watched with envious eyes as the midnight blue 2006 Mercedes Benz e350 pulled away into the night.

$$$

The drive three blocks to the house was a quiet one. Toya was secretly proud of her man at how he handled the situation. The way he stayed unruffled and composed was a turn on. As Ty parked the car, Toya's panties began to get wet with excitement from the thought of her and him being body to body. She didn't quite understand what this feeling was. She was no stranger to her womanly area. She spent countless nights arousing her own pearl thinking of this very moment, this very night. Toya had been pushing Ty to take her innocence for two whole years, but he always politely declined saying the same thing every time: *I got too much respect for you Ma. Let me get to know your soul, heart and mind before I explore your body.* She heard his voice in her ears. Just thinking about how caring and patient he was caused a flame between her legs that only he could put out.

The waiting game was what made tonight so special for her. She felt Ty was worthy enough to snatch her vCard and hold it in his back pocket forever. She knew once this was done there was no undoing it; he would indeed be her first. She heard all the depraved stories of what happened when girls give away their virginity to a *Mr. Wrong*. She trusted and loved Ty so much that she was willing to take this chance; she knew he would do her no wrong.

Once Ty unlocked the door to the apartment, she was hot on his heels turning him around kissing him fully. She placed her tongue deep into his mouth. She wrapped her arms around the nape of his neck as he lifted her up, her legs wrapped around his waist. Ty could feel her pussy throbbing through her sweats, begging for entry. As they kissed, he closed the door and locked it with her still wrapped securely in his arms.

Their tongues never stopped dancing to its own tune, their bodies craved one another. Carrying Toya, he walked into his bedroom. His dick was fully erect making an enjoyable thick nine-inch print in his sweatpants. He placed her onto the bed and then stepped out of his clothes. The contents that he just wore laid in a messy pile on the floor. Sneakers then sweat pants and then shirt. He stood in front of her with just his Burberry checkered boxers and a pair of white socks.

His chiseled, thick, rock-hard abs glistened under the low-lit room light. The muscular cuts right at his waistline were deep and distinct. Toya looked up and half regretted getting him started up. She looked at his body deeply and realized that he was all man. This wasn't no little ass boy she was letting take her virginity. Ty was a grown ass man. As she looked down below his waist, she saw his imprint through his boxers. *My God, please don't let him rip me in two*. Toya was interrupted from her thoughts by his voice.

"You want to strip for me or am I undressing you?"

Ty looked at her hungrily as he licked his plump, juicy lips and smiled. He loved showing off his deep dimples because he knew she treasured them; it was her weakness. Toya felt like she was in a shell, but she was ready to burst out; every emotion she felt right now was heightened. Ty looked at her with new eyes, sensing that after tonight their relationship would change forever.

Ty removed both of her sneakers from her feet as well as her socks. Her cute, chubby toes were dressed in a fresh paint of fire hydrant red. Ty lifted her lower body from the bed as he slowly removed her sweats from her waist, pulling them down to her feet and then tossing them onto his black, plush carpet. Toya sat up and removed her shirt, pulling it over her head. Her red lace bra held her already perky, nice, rounded breast higher up. She wore a nice pair of red lace panties to match.

Ty looked at her eagerly, anticipating how it would feel once he entered her virgin wetness. He pulled her panties from her lower half and tossed them onto the floor next to her shirt and sweats. Toya had goosebumps all over her body as Ty kissed her from her neck down to her waistline, leaving behind his sweet trail of saliva. The air conditioner hummed quietly in the lavishly decorated room as the two explored each other's bodies.

Ty's kisses reached her neatly shaved pussy lips. His mouth watered; he had to know what she tasted like. He started off slow and gentle. His warm breath blowing onto her clit drove her crazy.

"Mmm," she moaned in a whisper as she arched her back.

He then licked away like a thirsty man drinking from a faucet after hours of dehydration. His licks were slow and precise at first to savor the taste, then he picked up the pace. As she wrapped her legs around his neck, he dived in enjoying the fat, wet, sweet treat before him. Toya threw her head back as she moaned passionately.

"Ooooo, ahhhh Boo, it feels soooo good." Toya managed to get those little words out before her body trembled taking her through her first real climax.

She'd brought herself to the climaxing point time and time again, but the forced orgasms she had given herself in the privacy of her bedroom or in the shower were nothing like this. Ty licked all the juices that dripped from Toya's opening. His dick grew harder; he couldn't wait anymore. He had to be inside of her.

The clock read 12:03 A.M. Lying on top of Toya, Ty kissed her passionately. Every kiss he delivered drenched her skin with his love.

"Happy   birthday Ma."

Her body tensed up as it got ready for the entry of his hard, now nine-and-a-half-inch dick.

"Relax, baby girl. I'm not gonna hurt you. If it hurts, I will stop. Okay?" he said with worry in his voice.

Toya shook her head and bit her lip as she slowly opened her legs. She was ready.

Ty reached into his nightstand and began fumbling for a condom.

"No boo, please don't. I want to feel all of you."

Toya wanted to get the full experience of losing her virginity to the man that she loved. She heard an old tale that a condom took the feeling out of it. If she was going to lose her virginity to the man that she loved, she wanted to feel every moment of it to savor for later.

Ty closed the drawer back.

"Okay, before I nut, I'm gonna pull out, I promise," he said reassuringly.

Ty reached for his dick and placed his head right at her opening. He felt her wetness and warmth. Slowly he pushed inside of Toya's opening. The pain caused Toya to clench her teeth together tightly as she held in screams. Their eyes locked as he continued to push into her tight vagina. Once fully in and past her hymen, he fit perfectly like the last piece to a puzzle. Ty let out a deep moan.

"Mmmmm." He slowly stroked in and out of her now virgin-less pussy.

He rocked gently and carefully in and out of what was now his.

"Are you okay?" he asked as he stopped his strokes.

Toya opened her eyes and looked up at Ty. She wanted him to stop desperately but when she saw the concern plastered all over his face, she instantly became more relaxed and then spoke.

"Yes, keep going. Make me feel good baby," she said in an unsure manner.

Toya slowly wrapped her legs around Ty's waist. He continued his slow strokes, being careful not to put his whole dick in. *I'll save that for the next time*, he thought as he watched his glossy dick disappear and reappear in and out of her garden. A sensation she never felt before was building up; she felt pain from Ty penetrating her inner walls, but she still felt an enormous amount of pleasure.

She felt as if she had to pee. She tried to hold it, but she had to let it go. Ty increased his pace carefully, knowing by looking on Toya's face that she was about to climax again. His focus was pleasing her. It was her first time, so he showed not an ounce of selfishness. She was his; he had time to please himself in the future.

He wanted this to be special for her so that even if things went sour between them later in her life, she could never say that she regretted her first time.

"How does it feel Ma?" Ty asked in a hushed tone into Toya's ear.

"It feels good Boo," she answered as she bit her bottom lip and moaned.

Ty continued his slow strokes in and out. He maneuvered his hips in a circular motion while still thrusting Toya's tight walls.

"Oooooo Ty, I love you so much," Toya said.

"Oh shit! Ma, this pussy is the best."

A tear trickled from Toya's eye. She was completely fulfilled. Ty said that her pussy was the best. Toya was no stranger to knowing that before they were a couple publicly, Ty was the type of niggah to fuck around, A LOT. So, for him to say that she had the best pussy, she knew that she could have him whipped if she wanted.

They moaned together as Toya's body trembled again.

"Oh my God Tyshawn!" she screamed in ecstasy, reaching her climax for the third time. Ty felt his climax building from the base of his dick to the head. She sounded so sexy calling his name out like that. He still pumped in and out, making deep strokes until the end of Toya's climax.

Sweat beads dripped from his forehead and onto the bed sheets, but he continued to pump Toya's wet, warm, and tight throbbing walls.

"Latoya, I'm about to nut!" he said urgently.

"Nut in me, Boo!" she responded quickly.

Toya didn't know why she blurted that out. For one, that wasn't the plan, and secondly, she wasn't ready to be anyone's mother, but she thought this would make Ty happy and she lived to make him happy.

"Argggggggg .... Shittt!"

Ty's deep baritone vibrated the walls as he pulled out and let go onto the vacant spot on the bed beside Toya. Both their hearts were racing. *Damn, I love this bitch*, Ty thought as he looked down at his princess. She looked up at him with new eyes. Mentally, she was well beyond her years but now, tonight, she was indeed a woman.

Toya was confused. She told Ty it was okay to nut inside of her, but he still pulled out.

"I said it was okay," she said towards the back of Ty's head as he got up and retreated towards the bathroom to take a piss. Her eyes focused on his naked ass as he walked further and further away. He ignored her as he strolled into the bathroom and then closed the door behind him.

Toya sat up in the bed with a huge feeling of pressure in her lower abdomen. Streaks of blood painted areas of the beige satin sheets crimson. She got up from the king-sized bed and then examined it. It was a mess. She put on Ty's white t-shirt that was on the floor, and then stripped the bed of its covers. Because of her countless visits, Toya knew where Ty kept his sheets. She opened the bottom drawer to his chest drawer. She found a black, long, velvet jewelry box. She opened it and found a diamond covered, white-gold tennis bracelet engraved:

Forever my little Mama,

- T

She grinned knowing that this had to be her birthday gift. Hearing the toilet flush, Toya threw the box into the drawer, pulled out the satin black bed sheets and quietly closed it shut. Once the bed was made, she put on a fresh pair of panties and got back into bed. Her legs were too weary to wash tonight so she held that task off until the morning.

Her stomach was in knots, but she thought it was all worth it. Ty entered the room feeling different about the girl that laid in his bed before him. He realized that he was even more in love with her.

"I didn't hurt you, did I?" Ty asked with a concerned tone.

As bad as Toya wanted to say, *hell yea nigga!* She held her composure and didn't respond. Seeing the look of confusion on Toya's face and knowing his girl, he knew exactly what was troubling her thoughts, so he continued.

"I didn't nut in you because I don't want you to be my baby mama."

Toya seemed upset at his response, but she nodded in agreement. *What the fuck was I thinking anyways?* she thought. Sensing her slight frustration, he quickly continued.

"I mean, yea I want you to have my rug rats someday but no time soon, and plus I would want you to be my wife first."

Toya blushed at the thought of wearing a ring of assurance to the man that she loved. Ty turned off the light and then snuggled up behind Toya, wrapping his left arm over her waist tightly. Toya felt at ease as she laid wrapped in his embrace of protection. She stared at the digital clock on the dresser. It read 1:17 AM and then 1:18 AM, and then her eyes shut until the morning.

Chapter 4

"What the fuck you mean my shit not looking right? If anything comes up short, it's your ass!" Ty yelled through the phone just before he hung up angrily. He stood in the kitchen looking towards his bedroom; his heart felt whole-hearted as he watched Toya sleep peacefully. She looked so content. He couldn't wait for them to be moved in together. He stood fully dressed, with a long, black, velvet box in his hands. He wanted to just hurry up and give her the gift that he had purchased for her, but he decided to wait until the time was right.

He looked over into his living room and saw that her duffle bag was placed neatly onto the plush carpet. While still eyeing his bedroom's entry to make sure that she didn't wake, he carefully placed the velvet box into her bag. *That'll make her smile when she gets home,* he thought as a smile spread across his face. Ty left Toya sleep in the apartment.

He hadn't had his ear to the streets for one whole day, so he had to handle some business.

$$$

The bright rays from the sun awoke Toya from the best sleep she'd had in years. After rolling around in the sheets, she finally opened her eyes to see that Ty wasn't lying beside her.

"Ty?" she called out.

The echo of her morning raspy voice filled the vacant rooms of the apartment. She realized that she was totally alone. Getting out of the bed, she walked towards the bathroom to brush her teeth. While looking at her reflection in the mirror Toya realized that she looked completely different to herself. She looked more confident, happier, and a tad bit older. After taking care of her hygiene, Toya realized that she hadn't checked her phone since nine o'clock the night prior.

Wrapping a towel around her damp, silky hair, Toya went through her phone. She saw numerous random numbers texting *Happy Birthday.* She responded to some but the message from her mother and Leah that she was expecting just wasn't there. Frustrated that her mom and her best friend hadn't called or texted to say Happy Birthday yet, she got back into the bed, laid down and turned on the television. After calling Ty and getting no response, she figured he was busy. She decided to just watch TV and patiently wait for his return.

"And now to you, Stacy Grey."

A newscaster in the station said before the screen switched to a timid, frail white woman wearing a chocolate-colored pants suit. She stood in front of the camera apprehensively with a microphone close to her lips.

"Yes, thank you, John." She took a deep breath and then she continued, "I'm standing here in East New York on Pennsylvania Avenue where you can see that authorities taped off this section behind me. Police are trying to figure out who is responsible for the drive-by shooting that killed four innocent bystanders last night around eleven thirty p.m."

She paused to catch her breath and then continued.

"Some civilians are standing by lighting candles and saying prayers for those that we have lost. I will name them now," she paused.

"Raheem Grant, twenty-four years old." A picture was shown of a young man with a caramel face on the television. He looked so familiar to Toya. *Rest in peace,* she thought.

"Evelyn Waters, seventeen years old."

Toya looked at the television and felt sorry for the face that looked back at her. *She's one of them "hating ass bitches" from 1st period. Damn!* she thought. She knew Leah and the girl were somewhat close. Toya reached for her phone to call Leah. The heads up about Evelyn was needed. The reporter said another name that Toya was not acquainted with. Just as Leah's phone went straight to voicemail, Toya heard the woman say…

"And finally, Leah Ramos, she was only 18 years old."

Alarms rang off in Toya's ears, her whole head was sizzling, she didn't know what to do.

"This bitch got the wrong name," she screamed out loudly. Her thoughts were answered by pure fact once a picture of her best friend was plastered all over Ty's sixty-inch screen television. Toya kept calling Leah's phone hoping and praying that she would answer. Turning off the TV and flinging the remote, Toya let out a scream that only one of a broken heart could harvest.

Rocking back and forth in the center of Ty's bed, she cried. She wept like a baby for the regret she held in her heart and for the pain she felt for her best friend.

"Maybe if I would have stayed the night with Leah none of this would have happen," she mumbled to herself.

Toya cried for half an hour. Her screams and tears became whimpers as her eyes closed. She prayed that it was all a dream.

$$$

"So, was everything successful last night with that niggah Rah?" Ty asked as he sat at a table with his partner in crime, his day one niggah, Bleek.

"Shit went smooth like butter, hit a couple of crosshairs, but fuck it."

They toasted their shot glasses of VSOP to them getting revenge on Raheem, a local drug dealer that claimed he got robbed with twenty-five thousand dollars of their work on him. Ty and Bleek were both too smart to believe that, so they took Raheem's words as him stealing from them. Ty and Bleek were fair to everyone they allowed to sit at their table. Everyone ate equally so they despised greedy niggas.

Ty and Bleek both grew up in Bushwick. At the young age of fourteen they both decided that they needed a serious come up, so they went into the game together. Six years later, they were both successful in their hustle game. Although it was evident that Ty was the brains of the operation while Bleek was the muscle, at any given time they could switch hats and play each other's role.

"I really hope your shit wasn't sloppy, because you don't be giving a fuck," Ty said jokingly, knowing that his boy would hit anything moving just to hit his target.

"I mean… like I saw about four bodies drop, but fuck it. I know I got his ass."

After talking more business, Ty left to get back to Toya. He knew that by now she would be up with an attitude wondering why he was out so early in the morning.

Around the corner from his house, Ty stopped at the bodega to pick up breakfast for him and Toya. He called her phone to ask what she wanted but she didn't answer so he just got two orders of what he was having. Ty placed the food on the kitchen counter and wondered why the rest of the house was quiet. He walked into his room and saw that his television screen was shattered.

Toya was asleep. She was sprawled out in the middle of his bed with just a towel wrapped around her body and one around her head. She looked sexy to him, so he watched her sleep peacefully.

"Ma? What the fuck happened to my TV?" Ty put bass in his voice when he asked.

"Ma, wake up…"

He waited for her to respond as he tapped her gently on her thigh.

"Leah?" Toya mumbled as she whined. Ty had a look of pure confusion on his face.

"Baby girl, what's wrong?" he asked.

When Toya finally realized that the voice that was talking to her was Ty, she opened her eyes with tears welled in them.

"Ty, Leah's gone, she's dead."

Damn, Ty thought. It was no secret that he didn't care much for Leah, but he couldn't bear to see his Queen hurting. Toya assembled the little energy that she had left to explain to Ty how she saw the story on the news and how her best friend was shot and killed in East New York. Ty's thoughts started positioning bits and pieces of information together. *Bleek did business last night in East New York.* He prayed that his business had nothing to do with Leah's killing.

He wouldn't know how he would tell Toya that his street business brought death to her personally. Ty consoled Toya as he held her in his arms and told her that everything would be okay. With Ty, she felt safe and he knew that, so if he said that everything was going to be ok, that was what she believed. As she cried softly in Ty's arms she dozed back into a slumber. Although he wasn't tired, somehow Ty managed to doze off too.

Chapter 5

"That little heffa better be in a deep ass sleep," Kinsey mumbled as she walked the floors of her two-bedroom apartment. She called Leah's house numerous times and when there was no answer, she had begun to call her daughter's phone which rang out. She became angrier and angrier by the second wondering what the hell her daughter must have been up to. To calm her nerves, she turned on the television and began to clean up the house.

Lance rolled around in bed frustrated that his woman wasn't lying right beside him. Looking for the remote, he decided to turn from the music station and turn to the news. He watched with a raised eyebrow as the news reporter just stated the names of those innocently shot in a drive-by shooting the night before.

"Leah Ramos... Leah Ramos," he repeated the name lowly thinking that this Leah couldn't have been Leah, Toya's best friend. Once her young, eighteen-year-old face adorned the television screen the answers to his questions were confirmed.

"KINSEY!" he yelled with bass in his voice.

He knew that his good for nothing step-daughter was up to no ass good.

Her little fast ass. She wants to be grown huh? he thought as he yelled for Kinsey again.

"KINSEY!"

Walking at a fast pace from the bathroom, Kinsey responded in her sweetest tone, "Yes baby?"

Lance tried to keep his cool when he was about to open his mouth, but he couldn't hold in what he was about to say.

"Now, I am very much aware of the relationship that you have with your daughter. I try to put my foot down at times and be the father figure but no, you step right in and shut me out."

Kinsey looked confused as she listened to Lance speak with such seriousness in his voice. She shifted her weight to one leg as she listened nervously.

"Now last night I said don't let her ass stay the fuck out. I said make sure she brings her fast ass home. That's what I told you, right baby?" Lance asked as he rose from the bed. Walking towards Kinsey, his 6'2 frame hovered over her small 5'5 stature. He grabbed her shoulders gently and rubbed them as he continued. "Right baby?" he asked once more.

Kinsey thought about if the question was rhetorical or not. She remained quiet and just shook her head up and down to slowly agree with him.

"Okay, good." He kissed her on the side of her face and then continued, "Tell me this, why the fuck was her so called best friend found dead last night around eleven in East New York when she told you that she would be out to eat at Sammy's in the Bronx with the little bitch at that time?"

Kinsey's eyes shifted from left to right as she attempted to intake all this new-found information.

"So, once again I repeat, didn't I tell you last night that her little fast ass should have stayed home?" he asked. Kinsey wore the pure expression of shock, confusion and rage as she listened intently. Her daughter lied to her and made her look like a fool in front of Lance. *Maybe she's hurt? Na… she would have been stated as injured on the news. When Toya comes out of hiding, her ass is grass,* Kinsey thought.

He grabbed Kinsey by the throat as he spoke loud and clear, putting emphasis on every single word that he said.

"I told you that little bitch was no good, I told you she was sneaky and was hot in the pants. Her ass is probably out right now with some boy! See, you baby, you don't have what it takes to be a parent. You should have given her ass up years ago. You don't know how to discipline her ass. Since she wants to act grown, I will be the one to show her fast ass what it is to be a grown ass woman."

His emphasis on the word *I* rattled Kinsey's core. Lance's dick grew a little in his boxers as his grip around Kinsey's throat became tighter and tighter. The weak expression she wore on her face turned him on even more. Grabbing her closer to him, he threw her body towards the wall with force. As she fell towards the ground her body made a hard thud that echoed throughout the cozy apartment. Lance looked down at her with disgust.

"You call her ass and tell her to bring her ass home! Now go clean your stupid ass up!"

He retreated into the bed and laid down as if nothing happened, leaving Kinsey sobbing quietly on the bedroom floor.

$$\$\$\$$$

Slowly awakening from her inactivity, reality started to repeatedly hit Toya like a ton of bricks. Looking at the digital clock on the nightstand, she saw that it was one in the afternoon. Panic started to set in as she quickly remembered that she had told her mother that she was with Leah the night before. She checked her phone and saw only two missed calls from her mother. She felt somewhat relieved because she knew that her mother didn't care to watch the news on her days off. Getting home to see if she was in trouble or not became her priority. She had to temporarily push the mere fact that she had just lost her best friend to the back of her mind.

"Ty, wake up!"

Toya pushed and nudged the sleeping log next to her until he slowly started to come to. Sounding groggy and still halfway sleep, he spoke, "Hey, how you feeling?"

Jumping up from the bed and throwing on her clothes from the night before, Toya explained to Ty how she needed to get home to see exactly what her mother knew. After brushing their teeth, they headed out the door. The traffic-filled drive from Bushwick to Flatbush was a long one. As they slowly pulled up to her apartment building, Toya started to feel as if she was going to shit bricks. She became more serene when she saw her aunt sitting on the stoop smoking a Black & Mild.

Kelsey Greene was Kinsey's baby sister. Being only thirty-two compared to Kinsey's rising age of forty, she held a tighter knit relationship with her niece. Because of how young Kelsey acted and looked, everyone assumed she was Toya's older sister. Their resemblance was spooky. They both shared the same complexion, the same facial features, even the same doe-shaped, green-colored eyes.

Toya exited the car regretting even coming home because she knew that it was about to be static. "Check your bag when you get upstairs and text me," Ty yelled outside of his car's window. "Yo, wussup Ke," he managed to say as he chucked up the deuces and then sped off the block.

"So, you want to tell me what happened before you get upstairs?"

Kelsey put out her lit Black & Mild and patted the step beside her, ushering for her niece to sit.

Toya told her aunt everything, sparing no detail. She had that kind of relationship with her aunt where she could freely speak and not get judged.

"You're growing up and shit happens. Ty seems like he's good to you and that's all I can ask for. Just make sure he has a young, fine ass friend for me."

Laughing and playfully nudging her niece's shoulder, she tried to lighten up the mood as she continued.

"Your mother was very worried about you. Shit, I was very worried about you. So, when you go upstairs just have your shit straight, no stuttering no nothing, tell her the truth Toya."

Debating on if she should be honest with her mother or come up with some crazy story to cover her own ass, she took a moment to weigh her options.

"Did she see the news?" Toya asked her aunt with deep curiosity hanging on every word that left her mouth.

"Of course, she did. Why do you think I asked you what happened?"

Toya rose from the stairs and slowly walked into her apartment building. She was slightly starting to regret her prior night's encounters.

"Be honest," Kelsey yelled behind her niece as she sat sipping on her wine cooler allowing the summer's breeze to flow through her long natural hair.

$$$

The walk up the stairs to the third floor was a long one. Once in front of her front door, Toya placed her ear to the framed metal to try and listen to what was being said on the inside. When things seemed quiet, she stuck her key into the door. The walk down her long entry hallway was a swift one as she prepared for the worst.

"Oh, here she goes!" Lance spat from his mouth as he slowly started clapping. He brought a dramatic vibe to the room. His strong, manly stature rose from the plum-colored, suede sofa.

In no time, he made his way towards his step-daughter. The closer he got the more Toya could smell the Georgi Vodka that lingered on his breath. As he stuck his finger in her face, he spoke his words slowly and with much bass in his voice. "Tell me! Where the fuck you were last night?" he demanded.

Before he could continue his mini investigation, Kinsey interfered, "Lance shut up, this is for me to handle, not you!"

The closer her mother walked towards her, Toya could see her slightly swollen left eye, her busted eyebrow and the red colored bruises on her wrist and neck. It was obvious that they had been fighting in her absence, yet and still her mother's unique features still shined through the ass whooping that she was currently dressed in.

Her perfectly arched eyebrows complimented her high cheekbones. Although her hair was messy from being tossed around, her silky, neat cut bob with Chinese bangs made her cat-shaped hazel eyes look mysterious. Kinsey stood looking down at her daughter with her hand placed on her hip and her other hand pointed and placed in Toya's face.

"Think really long and hard before you answer my question because I already saw the news. Where were you?"

Toya shifted her weight from one leg to the other, a nervous trait she picked up from her mother.

Her nerves shook as she tried to think of exactly how she could explain what happened to her the night before. *Last night was magical Ma. I gave my virginity to the man that I love. Last night was everlasting and probably will always be embedded in my soul.* Her thoughts consumed her as a slight smile caused the corners of her mouth to rise upward. She knew that her mother wouldn't understand because her obvious disinterest in Ty was no secret.

Her aunt's words repeated in her mind. *Be honest.* She took a deep breath before she spoke, "I was with Ty, we didn't do any—"

Before Toya could finish the lie that she was about to release from her mouth, she watched her mother's freshly French manicured finger retreat into her hand and turn into a balled-up fist. Toya landed head first onto the hardwood floor.

The blow to her eye made it hard for her to see where the next hits were coming from. She was defenseless against her mother's blows.

"You were about to sit your ass in my face and tell a lie! You don't think that I know when you're lying! From when you first walked in this bitch, I knew ya hot in the pants ass was up to no good. I could smell the bullshit reeking off you."

Kinsey continued to kick, spit and claw at the young teen beneath her as she continued to speak. "So tell me what the fuck happened!"

Toya looked up at her mother and begged for her to stop. She felt her eye slowly swelling, and her neck burned from little scratches that tore her flesh wide open.

"Ma, please stop, Mommy, please," she begged and tried to plead with the vicious beast that stood above her.

Kinsey tried to stop herself numerous times. Deep down inside she didn't even think that she was upset that Toya stayed out. If anything, she was more upset that she was made a fool of in front of Lance. She slowly snapped from her mad rage when she heard the whimpering of her child. Sweat beads caused her already dismantled cut bob to frizz up. She stepped away from the beaten child on the floor and then she spoke, "Fuck your graduation. I'm not paying for shit, you won't be going."

Stomping down the long hallway towards the front door, Kinsey had to get some air. She needed to clear her head, so she walked across the hall to her sister's house to try and take her mind off things.

Chapter 6

Toya lifted her throbbing body from the hardwood floor and proceeded with the walk of shame towards the bathroom. On her way out of the living room, she looked over and saw her stepfather glaring at her. *I can't stand this niggah!* she thought as she felt every ache with every step that she took. Lance watched while he sat on the couch with one of his legs crossed over the other.

His lit blunt dangled from his lip. He just watched the whole fight and he was surprised that the encounter had turned him on. He inhaled the substance of the blunt and blew out the smoke as thoughts filled his mind. He knew Kinsey was never the woman for him. She was too weak, but what he had just seen from her a few moments prior proved that she still had some leftover spice that he had seen in her all those years ago. *Too bad her ass is showing all this sassy shit a little too late,* he thought as he frowned. His eyes were set on another woman now.

His thoughts drifted from his wife to his step-daughter. The tip of the blunt that dangled from his lip lit up a bright orange as he took another pull. He let the effects of the illegal substance and his thoughts take over him. *I knew she was out fucking.* He slightly got aroused at the thought of her in bed. Once inside of the bathroom, Toya cried and searched for her cell phone inside of her travel bag.

$$$

Ty maneuvered his way through traffic on the FDR drive making his way to the Bronx for a second time for the day. He needed to link up with his right hand Bleek. *Damn, B! Tell me you didn't hit shorty last night,* Ty thought as he listened to his blasting music. He was interrupted mid-thought when his phone began to ring.

Ring, Ring, Ring

"Yo?" he answered.

"Ty, please come back and get me!" Toya's voice spoke in a panic whisper as soon as he answered.

"Ma, hold on, tell me what happened."

Toya briefly explaining her encounters of when she got home. Ty agreed that he would come back to get her around ten that evening. With only four hours to spare, Toya told him that she'd shower, try to relax and stay clear of her mother until he arrived. She knew that this day would be the one where she would leave her home forever.

Ty circled Bleek's block for a while and when he found no park, he made a call.

"Ayo, niggah come downstairs, I'm in a hurry," Ty yelled through the phone as he patiently waited for Bleek to descend the stairs of his bachelor pad. Once rested inside of the cream-colored interior, Ty and Bleek embraced each other.

"Wussup boy, what was so important?" Bleek held a glare of confusion as he spoke.

"Aight, I have to be quick because I need to shoot back to Brooklyn to pick up shorty. Have you been watching the news lately? Well, after you handled that business in the East?"

Bleek shook his head from side to side. "Na, you know I don't keep up with that shit. What's going on?" Ty took a deep breath before he spoke. He hoped that Bleek was not about to confirm what he already knew deep down in his heart.

"When you hit Rah, did you hit any bitches too?" Ty asked.

Confusion and deep thoughts filled the car as the two men stared at each other in silence.

$$$

It took Toya over an hour to come to terms with the ass whooping that she had received. *I should have treated her like a bitch in the street,* she thought. Once nestled in the safeness of the bathroom and after talking to Ty, she decided that maybe nice warm beads of clean water would put her at ease. Going through her travel bag, she smiled when she saw the same long, black, velvet box that she had noticed the night before at Ty's house.

"I swear that man is my all," she whispered to herself.

There was no need to view the diamond-encrusted tennis bracelet again. Toya stepped her naked foot on top of the cold tub's floor. Once fully under the showerhead, Toya couldn't help but to wince in pain as the water bounced off her open wounds. As she washed her hair she whimpered; she cried hard. She was at a point in her existence where she hated her life. Right now, in this moment, the only thing she found joy in was her and Ty's relationship. Because of all the stinging from the soapsuds Toya ended her shower early.

Lance still sat legs crossed on the plum-colored sofa. As he took swigs of his booze and puffs from his blunt, he couldn't help but to think of how

Toya would perform in bed. Listening to the shower water running and then shutting off, he began to envision her naked, youthful body. Walking down the hallway towards the bathroom and the front door, he placed the chain lock on the front door. He knew that Kinsey didn't have the key, so he patiently waited.

$$\$\$\$$

Toya chuckled in her room while on the phone with Ty. As she lathered up her body with cocoa butter, he tried to keep her mind off what occurred earlier. He was doing a good job. Toya's room was one that most teenagers didn't even have. Her walls bore a soft pink and all the latest technology decorated her room, courtesy of Ty. Her aunt always covered and said that she purchased things for her when the real credit card swiper was Ty. Lance held his ear to the other side of the door as he listened to his step-daughter's conversation.

"I'm gonna be ready in a few. You still coming, right?" he heard her ask, so he busted opened the door.

"I know your ass isn't on that phone!" he shouted.

Toya was frightened. She jumped, which caused her to drop her phone because she decided that covering her goods was more important than holding the phone.

"Lance, get out! I'm getting dressed," she shouted.

Toya tried to regain her coolness as she grabbed her towel off her nearby bed and covered her body. Lance snatched at Toya's towel, freeing her perky breast from its confinement. The cool air from her room caused her nipples to harden.

"You wanted to be grown right?"

The look plastered across Lance's face when he asked his question told Toya that she had to fight to keep her body to herself.

"Ty, help me!" she screamed as she pushed Lance as far away from her as possible.

As expected, her little attempts had no effect on him. He forced her onto the bed as he released his brick hard eleven inches from his boxers. Toya squirmed and cried as she still tried to remove his two-hundred-and-fifty-pound frame from her body.

"Let Daddy get some of this sweet pussy you gave away already," he said in a drunken slur.

Ty listened on the other end of the phone and became immediately irate. Banging the wheel in frustration he glanced at the road ahead of him and realized because of the traffic it would take him at least an hour to get to Toya. Tears came to his eyes as he tried his hardest to not imagine what his girl was about to encounter. She was calling out his name for help, but the distance made it so that he could do nothing about it.

"Lance please, think about my mother."

All of Toya's pleas landed on death ears. Lance was too preoccupied with forcing his hardness into her tight walls. She cried as pain overwhelmed her. Lance sweated profusely as he pounded harder and harder. The more Toya cried out the harder he pounded.

Meanwhile on the other side of the door Kinsey opened the unlocked door but was halted in her tracks when the chain on the door stopped her. *What the fuck?* she thought as she pushed the door against the chain.

"Lance... Toya... somebody better open up this fucking door," she yelled as she peeked through the cracked entrance. She put all her concentration on her ears to hear if anybody was nearby. Toya heard her mother's voice and cried out to her.

"Ma! Mommy, please help me."

Lance looked down at the already beaten girl underneath him and punched her in her mouth knocking her unconscious. He pushed the bangs on the front door to the back of his mind as he continued to ram into her until her blood ran down his hairy legs. He felt his climax building so he grunted and released his seeds into her.

Ty hung up the phone and threw it to the back of his car as tears blurred his vision. The more he thought about what had just occurred, the harder he pushed his foot on the pedal. As traffic started to clear up, he turned his already fifty miles per hour into eighty in a split second. He drove recklessly. He prematurely cut off cars in other lanes as he tried his hardest to make it back to Brooklyn.

"Where the fuck is everybody?" Kinsey mumbled as she heard heavy footsteps approaching the door from the inside. Lance opened the door with a drenched t-shirt sticking to his abs. He had small red puffy scratches on his lower neck. Kinsey's Spiderman senses started tingling when she smelled sex in the air as she stepped into her apartment.

"Lance, where the hell is Latoya?" she asked.

Ignoring her question Lance headed towards the living room. Kinsey felt like something was wrong. Her heart began to beat rapidly in her chest once she looked at her daughter's closed bedroom door. She could hear her heartbeat in her ears.

"Maybe I should apologize for earlier. She's getting older and she's a good girl," she sighed out loud. Lance watched as Kinsey crept into her daughter's room.

She found her tucked in her covers sound asleep. She slightly smiled until she realized the pool of blood that the plush pink carpet was absorbing just right by Toya's bed.

Ma, Mommy, please. Help me.
Ma, Mommy, please. Help me.

The words replayed inside of Kinsey's mind as she tried to think of what she thought she heard to be true. Anger filled her eyes as she stormed out of her daughter's room and into the living room to confront Lance. Kinsey's face expression read pure rage as she stood just inches away from Lance's face.

"What did you do to Toya?" she screamed.

She tapped her foot against her hardwood floors as she waited for his response. Lance casually rolled up a blunt as he looked Kinsey up and down.

"What the fuck are you implying?" he asked.

He stood to his feet and glared at Kinsey like she had two heads.

"I'm no dumb bitch—" she screamed.

"You sure!?" he asked, cutting her off.

She continued, "I know I heard Toya calling for me, there's blood in her room and scratches on your neck. Did you touch my daughter?"

The bass in Kinsey's voice caused Lance to tremble a bit. He bit his bottom lip as he searched for an explanation that could make things better for him.

$$$

Toya awoke from her unconsciousness with sharp pains that plagued her lower abdomen. She visually searched frantically for her phone as she dug into her closet and retrieved her several duffle bags. She stuffed as many clothes in them as possible.

Once she received her phone, she saw twenty-two missed calls from Ty and four voicemails. Toya stopped mid-movement when blood trailed down her thighs. She hunched over and folded from the excruciating pains that she felt. She wiped the blood with her nearby towel and then tossed on sweats, a shirt and sneakers.

Kinsey and Lance held a deep conversation as their buzzer rung echoes throughout the silent apartment. Ty kept his finger pressed on the number fourteen hoping that Toya's mother would just buzz him up without asking who it was. After five minutes straight with no answer, he tried to remember the bell number for Kelsey's apartment.

The annoying sound of the buzzer woke Kelsey from her slumber.

"Now who the fuck is this?" she said groggily as she slowly arose from her bed while putting on her sheer robe.

"Who the fuck is it?" she yelled through the intercom. She twisted her neck sideways to read her kitchen's clock which read 12:53 AM.

"It's Ty, Ke let me up. It's about Toya."

Hearing the urgency in Ty's voice, she had no choice but to buzz him in. Ty rushed up the stairs to the third floor skipping two and three steps at a time. Once he met Kelsey in the hallway, he updated her on everything he had heard while on the phone with Toya. He could practically see the steam leaving her ears as he spared no details. Kelsey rushed back into her apartment to retrieve the spare key that she had to her sister's place.

$$$

Toya heard her mother's voice and felt a sense of comfort knowing that she had someone there that would hopefully have her back. She rushed out of her room. She let her feet follow her mother's voice. When she saw the anger plastered over her mother's face, she knew for sure that she had somebody on her side.

"So nice of you to have joined us. So, tell me why you think it's okay to blackmail my man into fucking you?" Kinsey's voice grew with every word she spoke.

Standing there with tears streaming and lightning bolt pains shooting through her abdomen she couldn't believe her mother. She misread her mother's angry expression. She thought she had someone on her side but to her surprise, she was the one that her mother was angry with.

"Blackmail? Ma, are you serious?" Toya asked as tears fell down her face.

"NO, bitch, are you serious? Since when was it okay to fuck my man, you don't pay a bill, you don't cook and you damn sure don't clean—"

Cutting her mother off mid-sentence Toya couldn't hold her composure anymore so she screamed, "YOUR MAN RAPED ME!"

Ty and Kelsey heard loud voices and commotion as they crept down the long hallway that lead towards the living room.

"He said that you would say that. You little bitch, after everything that I've done for you."

Kinsey lunged at her daughter. She grabbed her by her hair and banged her against the wall.

"You fucked my man!" she screamed.

Hearing enough, Kelsey raised her voice and spoke.

"Kinsey, get your ass off of Latoya, right fucking now!"

While holding both women apart to break up the scuffle, Kelsey continued to speak, "You need to act like a fucking mother! All you seem to do is put your daughter beneath this sack of shit!"

She yelled as she cut her eyes towards Lance. She looked at him with disgust while he sat calmly on the couch smoking his blunt. He looked completely unbothered and his coolness was pissing off the other male in the room.

Ty spoke through clenched teeth towards Toya while never taking his concentration off Lance. "Ma, you alright?" he asked.

Toya shook uncontrollably and gave no response. Kinsey broke the silence as she ice grilled her sister.

"You trying to tell me how to be a fucking mother! Tuh," she scoffed, "I don't think you should go there with me because what kind of fucking mother are you? You want to come save this ho, take her. Now it's finally your turn to play mommy."

The room remained quiet as Kelsey had a flashback...

Bang bang bang

Kelsey stood in front of her big sister's door pacing back and forth while a baby carriage sat on the floor beside her. Her sister was taking forever to answer the door.

"Ke what's the problem now?" Kinsey asked as she shook her head disappointedly. When she looked at her fourteen-year-old baby sister, she thought about how fucked up her life turned out. Ever since their mother had died from cancer the year before, Kelsey went on a downward spiral and the outcome was a baby.

"Please T, I need you to take her. You have your own place already, let me get myself together and I promise I will come back for her," Kelsey said quickly.

Kinsey looked down in the baby carriage and fell in love with the tiny, doe-shaped, green-colored eyes that looked back at her. Kinsey stood there and let minutes pass before she gave a response.

"Okay, give her to me. You have to promise me that when she turns sixteen you will come for her."

Kelsey thanked her sister over and over as she agreed to the promise with a pinky swear. Kinsey took the baby bag from her sister. Just before she closed the door she spoke, "Um, Ke what the hell is her name?"

Kelsey smiled as she replied, "Latoya, she has your middle name."

Present day...

Kelsey returned from her flashback with dismayed pupils. That vivid memory was almost eighteen years ago and every time she thought of it, her heart broke all over again. She looked at Toya and tears began to stream down her face involuntarily. Toya was a mirror image of Kelsey, a younger version of her. *Someone hurt my baby,* she thought as her tears streamed down her defined cheeks.

She lunged at her sister knocking her off her feet.

"I trusted you with her and look what the fuck you let happen. None of this was supposed to happen," she hollered.

Kelsey laid blow after blow towards Kinsey face as she spoke every word. Seeing his woman get the ass whooping of a lifetime, Lance decided to intervene.

Just when he rose from the couch, he was faced with the barrel of a long-nosed Desert Eagle. The look on Ty's face let Lance know that if he made any sudden movements, he would surely kill him.

"Sit yo' ass down before you take a permanent nap my niggah," Ty gritted through closed teeth.

The two women stopped their fight once they realized that a gun was exposed in the room. Ty spoke calmly but the seriousness in his tone let the whole room know that he wasn't playing games. Never taking his sight off Lance, he spoke to Toya.

"Baby girl, go pack your shit. Sorry Ke, she's coming with me."

Kelsey rose from the floor and when she did, she gave her sister one last good kick to the rib cage. A sly smirk showed on Lance's face and that alone sent Ty off the edge. Within seconds he had lost his composure.

"So, you think this shit is a game?" he barked.

Whack

"I don't think you want to play with me my niggah!"

Whack

"I'm two seconds away from killing yo' filthy ass!"

Whack, Whack.

The sound of crushing bone was all that was heard throughout the room as Ty hit Lance in the face with the butt of the gun repeatedly with each sentence he spoke. Lance's blood dressed Ty's fresh white t-shirt in red splattered dots. Ty's sweat dripped down his forehead as he took the safety off and pulled the hammer of the gun down. He was ready to shoot.

Hawk...twah

Ty spat on Lance's forehead and then forcibly pressed the barrel of the gun to his temple.

Kinsey cried out, "Nooooo, please leave him alone. Don't kill him!"

Ty looked like a mad man as he stood above Lance with gun in hand. Lance grunted and cried out, "Ah, come on man, spare me my life."

The more Lance spoke the angrier Ty became.

"Tyshawn, let's just go!"

Once those words left Toya's mouth, that was all it took to cool him off and spare the man in front of him his life. He backed away from the broken-nosed bum that lay in front of him and headed for the front door.

I'ma see this niggah again, and if I don't Bleek gone see his ass. R.I.P to this niggah, Ty thought as he descended the hallway steps with Toya and Kelsey following closely behind him. Once outside, the trio was all stuck in their own thoughts. A lot had just occurred that needed thinking. Ty grabbed the two duffle bags from Toya and placed them in the back seat of his double-parked car.

Kelsey looked at Toya deeply. She tried to read her as she searched for something to say, anything.

"Listen Toy—" Toya cut her off.

"Listen Auntie," she paused, "well you're not even my aunt. You're my fucking mother! There's nothing that I have to say to you. So please save it because in my eyes you are just as wrong as those two motherfuckers upstairs."

Toya never cursed at Kelsey before but in this moment, she had suddenly lost all respect for her. Tears fell down Kelsey's face as she listened to every single word that was said to her. Words filled with hate flew her way at a heartbreaking speed from her own flesh and blood, from her daughter.

Ty came back to the curb and reached out for Toya's hand.

"Please, I know you're going, just please, call me if you ever need anything," Kelsey said as she sobbed.

She was talking to Ty's and Toya's backs. Her statement fell on deaf ears. Ty opened the car door for Toya and waited for her to find her comfortable spot inside before he closed her door.

He then hopped in the driver's seat. He sat parked in the same spot for a while. His eyes watered just from looking at Toya's stressed and shattered image. He had heard what Toya said to her newly acknowledged mom just moments ago and in a way, he felt just as responsible. It was also his job to protect his lady and he felt as if he failed her too. *Never again,* he thought, *never will she ever be hurt again.* He gave her one last look over before he peeled off.

"Let's go home," he said quietly as he reached for her hand and kissed it.

Chapter 7

Six years later, 2012

Ty sat at a round table comfortably. Next to him was his right-hand man Bleek. A meeting was in session. The occupied warehouse in the industrial district of Williamsburg was one of their many stash spots. Their crew had put in a lot of work these past six years, leaving Ty at official boss status. He was king pin labeled. Just like his father in his younger days, he took over the entire tri-state area.

He was the supplier of Grade A fish scale product for all five boroughs including the entire New Jersey and Connecticut state. At twenty-six years old, Ty didn't just fill his old man's shoes, he surpassed whatever status his father had once had in the streets. Life for Ty couldn't have been any better.

He twisted his pinky ring, a habit he had when he found himself lost in his thoughts. His mental knobs turned rapidly as he looked around at the eight other bosses that sat with him. His crew, BS9, moved thoroughly in these streets. If it was territory that they wanted they took it, no questions asked. They were on some *get down or lay down*, State Property type shit.

"Listen, listen, listen, Pop, the matter of the fact is that you moved sloppy as fuck. Since when we leave bodies stinking in alleys?" Bleek asked sternly.

He interrupted Ty from his deep judgments. Bleek was second in command so at these meetings he voiced his opinion heavily, sometimes more than Ty. Pop, one of the nine men sitting at the table, listened to Bleek talk. He waited patiently to make his point.

"Yeah, you right Bleek, I did move sloppy. I could have dumped the bodies in the Hudson or buried them but bro, I had a nice piece of pussy waiting and I just got my car detailed. There was nooooo way them shits was getting close to my whip," Pop said.

Everyone at the table laughed at his sense of humor, even Ty. Pop was the group's jokester. He was the youngest of the nine men. After Bleek himself stopped laughing, he continued.

"Come on bro, now the N.Y.P.D sticking their noses around our business and shit," he paused and then continued.

"Some pig I got on payroll said some sack shit ass officer named Vasquez or some shit like that is tryna open a case against us. We have to move better."

Ty suddenly became intrigued. He cut Bleek off from his speech.

"Vasquez? Don't tell me that niggah from the 83rd precinct."

Bleek's eyebrow rose as he wondered what his boy was getting at.

"Hell yea, you know this niggah?"

Ty's mind drifted off as he remembered a night just six years ago…

"One of your tail lights is out. Do you mind giving my partner your license and registration?"

The Spanish officer seemed antsy. He seemed like the type to judge niggas like Ty. You know, the kind of cop that took power and authority to the head. Ty looked over and looked at the officer before he made a move. The nameplate he wore read: F. Vasquez.

Present Day...

"I remember that name from somewhere," Ty answered as he pushed the memory to the back of his mind.

Ty checked his iPhone and saw seven missed calls from Toya. *Damn, it's 2AM,* he thought. All the men were engaging in small talk.

"Aight y'all, let's wrap this up. Let's get the fuck out of here. All the numbers are still looking good. Yo Dro," Ty called out to another one of the bosses.

"Yo bro, wah gwaan?" Dro answered in his Caribbean accent.

"If you need to re-up hit Bleek's line, 'cause this weekend I'm gonna be out of town. Do you need anything right now before I leave?" Ty asked as he rose from his seat.

"Na bredren, everything cook a curry," Dro responded as he rose from his seat as well.

Ty squinted his eyes and then smirked.

"Son, what the fuck does that mean?" he asked.

Everyone laughed in the unoccupied space. Dro laughed as he spoke, "Bredren everything nice, I'm good." Ty shook his head as he still chuckled.

"I already know I'm in trouble when I get in the crib so y'all get y'all asses home," Ty joked as walked towards the lit exit sign.

$$$

Damn, she gone kill my ass, Ty thought as he sped from Williamsburg to Downtown Brooklyn. He had just come back from a business trip in the Dominican Republic earlier that morning and missed Toya's twenty-fourth birthday three days prior. He already knew that he had to make it up to her. He pulled up to his and Toya's home, a Downtown Brooklyn skyrise loft. He pulled into the underground parking garage and then made his way towards the elevators. He tapped his keys against his thigh impatiently as he watched the elevator skyrocket to the penthouse suite. Once he stepped off the elevator, he could hear loud music blasting from inside of his home. As he walked down the long, carpeted hall to his front door, the bass intensified. The sounds of Keyshia Cole filled his ears as he stuck his key into the door's lock.

I might as well have cheated on you

As much as you accused me of cheating

I might as well have lied to you

As much as you accused me of lying

I might as well have gone to the club

As much as you accused me of clubbing

Toya sat with her legs oiled and crossed one over the other, lady like, as she sang along.

"I should have lied… I should have cheated… Baby I should have went out to the club!"

She harmonized loudly with her eyes closed as she let the music wash over her heartache. She was sick and tired of Ty's business meetings, business trips, and missing in action antics. Yeah, the money he was making was great. She spent more money than she could count. But to her it seemed like the past six years had been nothing but just that, business moves, leaving her with less romance.

She caught herself at night in tears missing the actual love in their relationship. The steaming hot teenage love affair they shared years ago seemed to be extinguishing rapidly. Still with her eyes closed, she drank her Nuvo straight from the bottle. Once she opened her eyes, she saw her man standing in front of her with his Givenchy duffle bag in his hand and a saddened expression on his face.

He knew he had fucked up heavily this time. She eyed him intensively; age started to wear on him. His body was still fit but you could tell that he put on a couple of *getting money pounds*. He wasn't the skinny, muscular teenager that she had once knew. He was now a solid man. She watched as he rubbed his forehead, something he did when he was thinking of his next move.

The script bold letters on his wrist held her attention. The perfectly written tattoo read, *Latoya*, something he got years ago when they first moved in together. Back when he used to be her savior. She sang harder as she looked him dead in the eyes.

"Or maybe I… I should have played you, because you don't appreciate me noooooo. And I tried to stay down with you but you're making it hard for meeeee—"

She ended her singing once she realized that Ty had turned off her music. Once the space between them was a silent one, they just stared each other in the eyes. They weren't the same kids that met at a Bushwick block party; they were both grown now. Toya no longer held well-rounded C-cups; her breasts were now at a healthy D-cup size. She sat on the white leather sofa with just her long silk kimono robe on.

It was tied tightly just below her breast. Her natural long hair was in a messy high bun with Chinese bangs that slightly covered her eyes. With her thick, silky hair in the way, Ty still saw her green eyes as they pierced through his soul. She was drunk and livid.

"Baby look, I know—" he started, but she quickly cut him off.

"Shut the fuck up Tyshawn! I don't want to hear shit about you knowing anything. You knew my birthday was three days ago, didn't you?" she asked furiously as she uncrossed her legs and rose to her feet. She wobbled from her drunken state.

"I mean yea, Ma I knew—"

"I mean yea, Ma I knew, blah, blah, blah!" she said mockingly as she cut him off.

She took another swig from the bottle and then walked out of the living room's space and into the dining room, leaving Ty standing alone with his thoughts. She stood in front of the oversized windows that brought light into their eating quarters. She gazed at the Brooklyn Bridge as a tear fell involuntarily from her right eye. Once she heard his deep baritone, she wiped her tears away quickly.

"Just listen Ma, don't talk." He paused as he took a deep breath.

"I promised you years ago that I would take care of you. I literally just made it to a position where I can fall back and let someone else step in my shoes for a little while. Now it's time for me to show you how much I love you."

Toya's eyes welled with tears as she still stared fixedly out the window at the craftsmanship of the bridge.

Ty walked closer to his woman. Standing directly behind her, he wrapped one of his strong arms around her waist and leaned down to kiss the side of the nape of her neck.

"Are you gonna let me show you how much I still love you?" he asked sweetly.

She melted like butter in his embrace. Yeah, she was mad, but she loved this man with everything in her. "Yea," she responded almost inaudibly as she sniffled.

With his free arm Ty placed his hand in front of both him and Toya's faces. In his hand he held two plane tickets that read:

Departure: June 22nd, 2012 9AM
NEW YORK, JFK TO SAN JUAN, SJU

"We're going to Puerto Rico tomorrow?" she asked as she turned around and faced her man excitedly.

"We're going to Puerto Rico tomorrow," he confirmed.

"But baby, I didn't go shopping for us," she said worriedly as she pouted.

He smiled showing the dimples that she still loved. He knew that would be her first thought.

When it came to shopping, his lady tried to break the bank every time.

"I heard the malls out there are amazing," he said and then kissed her cheek.

He left her with a huge grin and her thoughts. A vacation wasn't going to completely fix the broken bond they now had, but it was indeed a start.

Chapter 8

"Ladies and gentlemen, welcome to Luis Muñoz Marín International Airport. Local time is 12:57 PM and the temperature is 87 degrees. For your safety and comfort, please remain seated with your seatbelt fastened until the captain turns off the Fasten Seat Belt sign…"

The flight attendant in a chipper voice then proceeded to repeat the landing message in Spanish over the loudspeakers. Toya looked over at Ty with a bright smile. They had made it their destination safely.

"Come on Ma, grab your purse and shit."

Ty loved to travel, he just hated to fly. He took the last swig of his Corona. He placed the bottle in a plastic bag on his way leaving out from the first-class section. Once they were inside of the airport it was chaotic; finding their way to the taxis was a mission of its own.

"You guys don't have a bag?" the taxi driver asked in his heavy Spanish accent.

"No Papa," Toya answered as Ty helped her get into the van.

"Take us to the Ritz-Carlton in Carolina," Ty said as he found his comfortable spot in his seat. He was ready to kick back with his lady and make the best out of this five-day vacation.

Toya looked outside of the window as their ride sped on the highway. She watched the palm trees as they passed by. She felt like this was just what she needed, new scenery. Back home she didn't have any friends, so she occupied her time with online classes, shopping, and drinking wine.

Her eyes became heavy, so she decided to take a little nap.

"Wake up beautiful," Ty said as he kissed Toya's sleeping lips.

"Huh?" she said groggily, as she slowly opened her eyes.

Once her eyes were open, she was in awe at how beautiful the hotel was. The front entrance was decorated with guests all in summer attire. She couldn't wait to get upstairs and change into her Fendi bathing suit.

The couple walked through the lobby hand in hand as they headed for the elevators. Once inside of the elevator Toya kissed her man passionately. He grabbed at her True Religion jean booty shorts. He needed to have her now.

Ding

The elevator's bell went off indicating that they had reached their destination, the penthouse. Toya knew that the room was lavish just off knowing her man. Whenever they traveled, he always lived how he lived at home, to the fullest with no monetary limit of course. Once he unlocked the door with the keycard, Toya's eyes began to water.

The view that the room had overlooked the ocean. A sense of serenest overcame her.

"Yea, I'm gonna enjoy this vacation," she said lowly as she closed the door behind her. She then made her way to the bathroom. It was time for them to freshen up so that they could hit the mall.

$$$

"Vasquez, where's your partner? Get your ass in my office, now," the sergeant said to one of his officers. Frank Vasquez had just walked back into the precinct from beat walking through one of Bushwick's crime hot spots. *Damn, I can't get a minute off my fucking feet without him busting my chops,* he thought as he walked towards his sergeant's office.

"Yes Sergeant," he said as he stuck his head inside of the office.

"Come in, come in, where's Blackwell?" he asked as he pointed to one of the chairs that sat on the other side of his desk facing him.

"I have no clue," Vasquez answered honestly as he took his seat.

"Well listen, I'm only gonna say the shit once, you'll just have to play messenger."

The sergeant took a sip of his coffee and then continued.

"I see that you're following the BS9 case. How do you feel about headlining it?"

Vasquez's eyes lit up; this was the opportunity that he was waiting for.

"You want me to be the leading investigator on that case?" Vasquez asked with his tone dripping in disbelief.

The sergeant smirked.

"If you want me to give away this opportu—" Vasquez cut him off immediately.

"Hell no! I mean no Serg, I'll gladly accept."

Vasquez sat back in his seat as his mind wandered. *This is exactly what the fuck I've been waiting on. She is going to love this,* he thought as his mind shifted from work to his wife.

"Um Vasquez?" the sergeant interrupted his officer's thoughts.

"Yes Sergeant?"

"Get the fuck out of my office."

Frank smiled as he stood and exited the office. This was his time to change his status in his employment. He was tired of beat walking, he was ready to move up in the ranks and if things went smoothly this would for sure give him next level status.

$$$

Bleek drove through the hood confidently; in Ty's absence he had to step up. Today was the day that Ty would normally pick up all the money from their several cash spots spread all over Brooklyn. The sun bounced off Bleek's candy paint as he rode slowly through Bedford Stuyvesant. Just as he drove past Fulton and Utica Avenue, his phone went off. He turned down his music to pick it up.

"Yo," he said loudly through the phone.

"So, you just gonna drive past me like that?" a woman's voice asked on the other end.

Who the fuck? he thought as he looked down at the number.

"Who this?" he asked.

"Eternity," she said seductively.

A smile spread across Bleek face, as he turned his car around. He always enjoyed his time with Eternity. She was his little shorty. It bugged the shit out of him that she never wanted to make it official, but he played her game for a few months now. As he drove up Utica Ave, he saw her standing right outside of Smurf houses. The maxi dress she wore hugged her shapely thighs. He pulled over and waited for her to get in the car.

"Hey Babe," she said as she leaned over and kissed him gently on his cheek.

"What's up with you Shorty?" he asked as he looked over at the pretty girl next to him. Her round cheeks and pudgy nose complimented her naturally thick eyelashes. Her full, soft lips held a tiny shade of lip gloss.

"Ain't shit. What are our plans for today?" she asked. That's one thing he loved about Eternity; she incorporated herself in his plans always.

"Gotta pick up some dough, you down?" he asked.

"Of course," she said as she put on her seatbelt.

Bleek peeled away from the curb and headed straight to Flatbush, the first money spot.

Chapter 9

Ty and Toya walked hand in hand on the soft, crystallized sand. The substance in between her toes felt exhilarating. They watched as the sun set, turning the once blue sky into a purple and orange mix. This was day two of their vacation, and it felt like time was moving too fast. The day prior, they spent their whole ante meridiem buying, eating and drinking whatever their eyes had a taste for.

Toya lifted her oversized Gucci shades from her eyes to get a better look at the sunset.

"You know this is nice," she said with her focus fixated on the sky above.

"It is," Ty agreed.

"It's actually nice to walk around and not have to worry about having a burner on me," he continued as he took a pull from his blunt.

He passed it to Toya allowing her a chance to indulge in his current state. She took the swisher wrapped cannabis and inhaled deeply. *Damn,* she thought as she began to cough profusely. Ty laughed as he patted her back. "Take it easy little baby. You can't be inhaling exotic shit like that."

"Shut up Boo," she said as she tried to catch her breath. With a few more puffs she was just like Ty, high as a kite. They walked slowly back to their hotel room. Their dinner reservation at Zesty Restaurant was scheduled for eight p.m. As they reached their floor, they both headed straight for the shower. Tiny grains of sand fell from their bodies as they walked.

Ty looked over at Toya's mahogany body and his dick slowly began to grow in his Gucci swim trunks. Her body looked sculpted. Her thick, oiled down thighs jiggled as she took steps towards the walk-in shower. Her perky, voluptuous breast complimented her pudgy abdomen. The slight chill around them caused her chocolate nipples to stand at attention. The right side of her hip and upper thigh wore a garden full of lotus flowers. The pink, red, blue and purple colors mixed well onto her skin tone.

In the middle of the artistic piece in cursive letters spelled the name: *Tyshawn.* He watched as she took her natural hair out of its messy bun, allowing the silky strands to fall at her shoulders. She opened the glass swinging door to the shower and looked back at him as she played in her mane.

"You coming or not?" she asked sensually.

Ty dropped his swim trunks to his ankles, showing off his standing soldier. His dick throbbed as he joined Toya. Inside of the shower the steam accumulated quickly once Ty closed the door behind him. Toya sat on the stoned bench in front of one of the four showerheads. The water beads bounced off her body as she gently stroked her thighs to get the sand off them.

She looked at her man as she opened her legs and let the water travel from her inner thighs to her bald haven. The stare they had was deadlocked. She never took her sight off him as she changed movements. She reached down and began to fondle her jewel. Her square-shaped nails were coated in a cotton candy pink.

Ty reached down and grabbed his manhood as he watched his lady please herself. He stroked his throbbing penis slowly, and as it blossomed in his hand Toya began to moan softly.

"Mmmm," she hummed as she inserted one finger into her opening. Her green eyes looked deeply into Ty's brown ones. The same finger she just used to please herself she let grace her full lips. She sucked all her own juices from her finger's tip. Ty couldn't take it no more. He walked over to Toya and stood directly in front of her. His penis and her face were eye to eye. She sat more comfortably on the bench as she took hold on Ty's manhood.

She placed his blossomed, mushroom-shaped head into her warm mouth, and it drove him crazy. She sucked effortlessly. Saliva dripped from her mouth as she picked up her pace. Ty grabbed a handful of her hair as he guided her head back and forth on his shaft. "Yea, baby," he moaned as she deep throated all of him. He pulled his dick out of her mouth and looked down at his glistening pride.

"Stand up and turn around," he ordered.

Toya stood up from the bench and did what she was told. She placed her hands on the shower's cold stone wall. Ty grabbed hold of her juicy rear end and played with her ass cheeks, jiggling and slapping them repeatedly. Ty reached down and slapped her ass with his dick, teasing her.

"Please Daddy, put it in," she whined as she looked back at her man. Ty grabbed Toya's shoulder from the back and slowly slid into her opening.

His deep, long strokes drove her to insanity as she creamed almost instantly. Their moans filled the shower as the warm water beat off their bodies. The slapping noise of Ty's balls hitting Toya's pussy lips echoed throughout the shower. Toya put one of her feet on top of the bench and arched her back to allow Ty deeper access into her garden.

"Oh? That's what you want to do?" he asked as he gave deeper more forceful strokes.

"Oh my God, yes Daddy!" she screamed as she began to throw her ass back, matching him thrust for thrust.

Ty pulled his dick out of Toya and then sat on the bench. Like a rehearsed dance routine, she already knew what he wanted, her elite cowgirl skills. She sat facing him and then squatted, sliding his dick back into her walls in the process. She wrapped her arms around the nape of his neck as he grabbed hold of her ass cheeks. She bounced up and down as she arched her back. Each stroke put her and Ty closer to their climaxing point.

"Ahhhh," she moaned as her bouncing intensified.

The couple kissed passionately as they grinded their love into one another.

Their tongues danced in each other's mouths. "Keep going baby," Ty instructed as he slapped Toya's ass aggressively. Their moans sang in unison.

"Get up, I'm about to nut," Ty said sternly.

"No!" Toya shouted as she bounced up and down harder. Ty scooped up both of Toya's ass cheeks and lifted her 140-pound frame swiftly. His deep moan vibrated the glass walls as he let his kids spill onto the stone floor beneath them.

He stood under the showerhead with one hand on the foggy glass wall. The couple both attempted to catch their breaths.

"I want a baby, boo," Toya said sadly as she began to wash her body.

"I know, just not right now Ma," Ty said as he took the soap from her and lathered up his rag.

$$$

Zesty Restaurant was one of Carolina's top hot spots. The purple lights danced on the porcelain tiles. The smell of fine cuisine could be found in the air and the view was to die for. The ocean waters hitting rock could be heard in the distance. Following behind the hostess, Toya led the way to their table and Ty followed closely behind with his hand on her lower back. Toya's purple Bebe maxi gown flowed as she strutted, one foot in front of the other. Her strap up, gold, metallic Fendi heels complimented her vibrant sheer dress, the low v-cut and two thigh splits showed off her assets.

Men's eyes shifted as the couple walked towards the back-balcony section. Ty's button up white Gucci shirt, white G Star cargo shorts, and white ups were fresh to death. His yellow gold earrings and Cuban link chain matched his iced out, gold pinky ring. Once they reached their booth they started off with drinks. Toya ordered a Pineapple Piña Colada while Ty settled with Hennessy straight on the rocks.

Ty watched how daintily Toya sipped on her drink. *I'm gonna make her my wife,* he thought.

"What? I got something on my face?" Toya asked as she grabbed a nearby napkin.

"No, you're just beautiful. That's all," he said with a huge grin on his face.

His bone straight teeth all showed, they glistened under the tropical-colored lights. The waitress came to their table with a bottle of champagne in a bucket of ice. "What's this for?" Toya asked as she thanked the leaving waitress.

"This baby girl," Ty started as he grabbed the bottle and popped the cork, "is the start of new beginnings."

He took two flutes and filled them up to the top. He handed Toya a glass and then looked her in her eyes. "When we get back home, I want all of our days to feel like this, stress free, loving and peaceful."

Toya was about to take a sip of her champagne, but Ty stopped her.

"Aht, aht, aht, not just yet," he said as he reached into his cargo shorts side pocket.

He placed a baby blue ring box onto the table and then slid it in front of Toya. Her eyes began to water instantly.

"Also, when we get back home, I'm gonna need you to start wedding planning," he said as he winked at his lady and then nodded his head towards the box on the table. Ty gave his signal to the DJ with a simple head nod. The sounds of Case filled the entire establishment as Toya slowly reached for the ring box.

Guess what I did today
Those were the words I said to you
It was last May, don't know the exact day
In my hand there was a ring
And you told me that you loved me
More than anything in your life
So I asked you would you do me
The honor of being my wife

Toya opened the box to see a white-gold and purple sapphire, her birthstone color, diamond-encrusted, 18k engagement ring.

When she looked up at Ty with tears in her eyes, she could see that he was already crying. It wasn't one of those ugly cries but one where tears just slowly slid down someone's face. The king of New York was wearing his heart on his sleeve for the woman that he loved. A ruthless man in the streets that held no remorse was showing his inner boy to the woman seated across from him.

"Your protector, your best friend, till my humble life is ended and time begins again," Ty talked along with the playing song as he looked his woman dead in her eyes.

He allowed his tears to flow freely. At this point Toya was crying also. She reached over the table and whispered in Ty's ear.

"Yes, I will marry you, now put my ring on my finger." She wiped the tears from his face as she kissed him over and over. Ty reached for the box and placed the ring on her finger. *Perfect fit,* Toya thought as she allowed Ty to wipe her falling tears.

The other guests in the restaurant began to clap for the exquisite couple. Ty lead Toya to the dance floor so that they could slow dance. She had two left feet but in this moment, it didn't matter. She could step all over his toes and he would still be smitten by her, he would still be madly in love.

Couldn't we be happily ever after?
We could be strong together for so long
Couldn't we be happily ever after?
Leaving you never till forever's gone

Toya placed her head onto Ty's shoulder as she let his feet guide her. She just knew that she would be waking up shortly, so she made the best of the moment. *Mrs. Latoya Chanel Barnett,* Ty thought as he inhaled the intoxicating aroma that Toya's hair held. Now that business was great, Ty knew that he had to get and keep his love life in a blissful place.

Chapter 10

"Where you been hiding?" Bleek asked as he stuffed his face with white rice, chicken and broccoli from his nearby Chinese Restaurant.

"I've been tryna get me together," Eternity answered as she took a tiny bite from her egg roll. She sat Indian style on Bleek's suede black sofa with nothing but one of his white t-shirts on.

"I want to leave New York. I'm tired of this state," she confessed.

Bleek listened closely to the beautiful girl beside him. He had to silently admit that he was growing tired of New York too. Ty was about to open up shop out in Fort Lauderdale and Bleek was heavily considering running things out there. *It's time for some new scenery,* he thought as he continued to eat. He wanted more than what New York life had to offer.

Being so close to Miami would feel like heaven to him. He had some family out there. *Maybe it's time for a change.* Bleek's thoughts flew out of the window once he saw the mocha beauty in front of him taking off his oversized white tee.

"What you doing Shorty?" he asked as he wiped rice from his face.

"What it look like?" she said bluntly as she sashayed feline-like towards him.

Instantly, he had become aroused. He sat his platter of Chinese food beside him as she climbed onto his lap. She kissed his chocolate neck passionately. Just as the couple got into the swing of things Bleek's phone rang loudly.

"Yo," he answered with an annoyed tone.

"Meet mi at di spot," a voice said before the line went dead.

There was no need for Bleek to play investigator, he already knew who was calling his phone. Dro's accent was easy to pick up from anywhere. He assumed his boy needed some more work.

He heavily regretted ending his night early with Eternity, but there was money to be made.

"Listen E," he said as he lifted her off his lap, "I have to make a run really quick. You're welcome to stay here until I get back."

He hoped that she would take his invitation but knowing her, she was always on the move.

"Na, I'm good. I'll just head out with you so you can drop me home," she said as she began to gather her belongings and get dressed. Bleek just shook his head as he watched her get herself together. *This girl hates being tied the fuck down yo.*

$$\$\$\$$$

"Do we have to leave?" Toya asked, her tone laced in depression.

"Unfortunately, we do," Ty answered with the same exact vibe. Earlier that day the couple explored the wonderful wonders of Old San Juan.

They walked for hours observing the scenery. Toya loved how she was bringing out a different side to her man, his younger side, the side she had fallen in love with.

She enjoyed her activity-filled day. They screamed I love you to one another as they zip lined through the rainforest. This vacation was exactly what their relationship needed, a break from the fast life with more focus on the intimacy of their relationship.

This was their last night in Puerto Rico and of course they spent it on the beach. They sort of made this like a tradition for themselves. When the sun set, they found the perfect spots on the sand to enjoy the view. Ty lay on the oversized beach towel with his arms behind his head while Toya lay on his chest.

Her hand fondled his abdomen showing off her new engagement ring. She gazed down at the diamonds as she thought about how life would be for them once they returned home. *I really hope we can stay on this path,* she thought as she kissed his tatted chest.

"Watch out Ma," Ty said as he sat up and stood to his feet.

"Boo, where you going?" Toya asked as she sat up to let him get up.

"It's not where I'm going, it's where we're going."

Ty picked up Toya and then began to run towards the water.

"No! Ty what are you doing?" she screamed playfully as she tried to kick out of his hold.

"Let's live Ma," he screamed excitedly as he ran into the water. The cool water splashed against their bodies. "Babe, no, your watch!" Toya couldn't stop the laughter from leaving her body. She didn't know what had gotten into her man, but she loved every minute of it.

"Girl fuck this watch," Ty said as he allowed the sea's water to splash into his Breitling watch.

Toya wrapped her arms around Ty's neck and turned her body towards him, an attempt to block the splashes from the waves.

"You're crazy Mr. Barnett." Toya stared into his eyes as he held her tight.

"But you love it Mrs. Barnett."

She reached in to kiss his full lips. This was something that they both knew; they were crazy for one another.

After a few more moments of splashing each other in the ocean they made their way back to their towel. On the journey back, Ty slapped Toya's ass. "Boy you better stop before you start some shit," she said flirtatiously. The couple got back to their hotel room, showered and was back out the door within the hour. Since tonight was their last night on vacation, Ty decided that they had to go clubbing.

Code Bar & Lounge was their hot spot for the night. The line outside of the establishment spread down the block but of course being V.I.P. patrons, Ty and Toya walked straight to the front of the line and were allowed access. The inside's atmosphere showed true to its roots, Puerto Rico. The Latin music vibrated the walls of the establishment.

Spanish princesses twirled around in their salsa gowns as they ticked their waistlines to the beat. Toya watched amazed as she followed Ty's lead straight to their V.I.P. section. Once they reached the back of the club, an attendant dressed in a black mini skirt with a black corset pulled back a large, burnt orange silk curtain to their booth. The booth's table was covered with complimentary champagne bottles.

"My name es Mercedes, look for me if ju need anything," the attendant whispered in Toya's ear. She then sexually licked Toya's earlobe as she placed a peppermint case in her hand.

Ty grew a hard one in his slacks as he watched the scene unfold before him. To his surprise, Toya's reaction was a cool one. Once they took their seats, Toya opened her hand to reveal the silver case that Mercedes had given to her.

"What, she gave you ecstasy?" Ty asked curiously.

"Of course not," Toya answered quickly as she opened the case.

Twelve colorful, small, round tablets with smiley faces on them filled the case. Ty smirked at his correct accusations.

"So, what's up Ma?" he asked as he licked his lips and then continued, "we gone make our last night in Puerto Rico one to remember?"

Toya smiled sinisterly as she placed one of the pills onto the tip of her tongue and then leaned over the table to kiss Ty passionately. The purple tablet slipped from her mouth into his, he chewed it, knowing that the effects would hit him harder and faster.

Toya reached into the mint case and retrieved one for her. After a few Coronas and margaritas, Ty and Toya had begun to feel the effects of the alcohol and drugs; the music was much more intensified. Mercedes, their waitress, came back to their table with another round of drinks. Toya couldn't help herself from looking at her body. She never looked at another woman sexually until now.

Mercedes' voluptuous Double D sized breasts filled her corset. When she bent over in front of Toya to place their drinks onto the table, her caramel areola became visible. Toya's mouth practically watered. For the first time in her life, she wondered what a woman tasted like.

Ty sat back puffing on his hand rolled cigar as he watched everything. He could tell by the look in his lady's eyes that she was rolling. Toya licked her full lips and then bit down on her pointer finger. Her engagement ring glistened under the club's lights. "Listen, Mercedes," Toya said in a very relaxed tone. "Yes Mamí," Mercedes answered as she leaned down to become ear level with Toya.

She gently played in her hair. Instantly, Toya creamed in her thong. The feeling of Mercedes' manicured nails massaging her scalp turned her on so bad. She felt as if she couldn't control her body. She cupped Mercedes' chubby cheek and then kissed her passionately.

The two women's tongues danced in each other's mouths. On the other side of the table, Ty's mouth could have caught flies. If he thought he had a rock-hard dick before, he was wrong. His manhood stood at attention as he watched the two ladies kiss like skilled lovers.

"My name is Toya and that's Ty. You want to leave with me and my fiancé?" Toya asked as she cupped Mercedes' round ass.

"Yes," Mercedes answered honestly as she bit her bottom lip.

Ty couldn't believe that he had just witnessed his woman bag another woman for them in front of him. This by far had to be the biggest turn on that he had ever encountered. Toya stood from their booth and stumbled slightly from her intoxicated state. Ty stood and then led the way for the ladies to follow.

Outside, a black, tinted 2012 Maybach 57 was waiting. As soon as the driver saw the trio exit, he rushed to open the door for his passengers. Once inside the isolation of the back seat, Toya and Mercedes began to kiss passionately. On the drive back to the hotel, the chauffeur occasionally snuck peeks through the cracked partition.

Ty smirked once he noticed the driver watching their show. He parted with three hundred dollars from his designer slacks' pocket once they reached their destination.

"Have a good night sir," the driver said as he closed the door behind the trio.

"Come on man, you see them? My night is gonna be more than good," Ty said as he chuckled.

He proudly showed off the two beautiful women on his arms.

Inside of the elevator, Mercedes and Toya kissed all over Ty's neck. The two women favored one another in body build. Like Toya, Mercedes was short and thick in the thighs and ass area and she carried big breasts. The only difference was her stomach was toned and her caramel complexion was a direct match to Ty's.

Her hazel, curly locks complimented her cat-like shaped hazel eyes. A beauty mark right above her nice full lips enticed both Ty and Toya. Ty looked down at the two ladies and thought of the many ways he could handle the two fun sized women. The elevator bell went off indicating that they had reached their floor.

Once inside of their lavish hotel suite, Toya opened the mint case and gave everyone another ecstasy pill. Her taste buds danced at the mcre thought of what Mercedes tasted like. She grabbed the caramel beauty's hand and led her to the bed. Ty took a seat on an idling chair nearby and just observed.

Toya pulled her orange sundress over her head and came out of her black Giuseppe heels. She kissed Mercedes' neck while removing her corset straps from her shoulders. The light from the stars was the only thing that illuminated the dark room.

Across the room, Ty lit the blunt he had just finished rolling. The auburn hue from the lighter swayed as it lit his drug of choice.

The two women were so into undressing one another that they hadn't even noticed that he turned on the stereo. The soft tunes of Trey Songz played through the speakers that were placed all over the suite.

This right here's a panty droppa! Whoaaaa
This right here's a baby maker.
Can I sing my song?
If you up in the club tryna get a rub
Then you need to tell the DJ to put this on
Put put put this song put this song on

Now stripped down just to her underwear, Mercedes stood in front of the couple in just her purple lace bra and thong. The pill she took just moments ago had begun to sink in. Her juices slid down her thighs as she kissed Toya. Toya took off her black lace bra and thong and then laid back onto the bed.

Mercedes crawled on top of her and covered her body in kisses. She licked her navel as she began to place kisses lower. Toya opened her thighs, giving Mercedes easier access to her waxed treat. Mercedes blew warm air onto Toya's clit which caused her to moan lightly.

"Mmmmm."

Across the room, Ty placed his blunt into the ashtray and began to undress himself. Once he was completely naked, he stroked his manhood. It began to grow quickly in his palm. Mercedes allowed her full lips to nibble on Toya's southern lips. She opened her mouth and flicked her fat, thick tongue quickly against Toya's clit.

"Oh my God," Toya moaned as she reached down and grabbed Mercedes' dome. She guided Mercedes' head and played with her thick curls as she feasted.

Hearing Toya's moan and watching another woman with her ass up pleasing his woman drove him to his peak. He was ready to dive his inches into wetness. He stood behind Mercedes and watched as she dug her fingers into and licked his woman's pussy.

Him and Toya locked eyes, she bit her bottom lip and then nodded her head, giving him the okay to enter Mercedes. After grabbing protection from the nightstand and securely wrapping his manhood, Ty grabbed the Spanish Mamí by her hips and crouched down to enter her. Mercedes's tight walls gripped Ty's dick.

"Oh shit," he moaned as he guided his dick into her. Mercedes stopped eating pussy to moan out in pleasure, "Ahhh Papí."

She grabbed Toya by the thighs and dove back in. The music filled room began to fill with moans from the trio. Ty picked up the pace with his strokes. His balls slapped roughly against Mercedes clit. He bit his lip as he stroked in and out. Feeling like he was about to climax, he pulled out and let the ladies trade positions.

I'm about to show her ass how grateful I am for her, Ty thought as he watched Mercedes and Toya change positions. Toya arched her back just how Ty had taught her. Being her first meant that he was her mentor. He was the teacher and for every lesson she listened intently and when it was time to be tested, she was graded with five stars every time. She knew how to please her man.

What she didn't know was how to please a woman. She had never eaten pussy before, but she was a fast learner. Ty whispered in her ear as she kissed Mercedes on the inner thighs.

"Lick her how you lick my dick Ma."

He kissed Toya on her neck and prepared himself to enter her.

Mercedes' pink, fat pussy glistened in front of Toya's face. Toya closed her eyes and licked away at Mercedes.

"Yesss Mamí," Mercedes moaned as she grabbed the sheets.

As soon as Mercedes came, Ty shoved his entire dick inside of his wet wifey.

"Ahhh Daddy," Toya moaned loudly.

"Don't stop eating that pussy!" he ordered as he gave deep, hard strokes.

Toya shoved her entire face into Mercedes' crotch. She massaged her clit with her nose while licking her opening with her tongue.

"I'm about to cum Toya," Mercedes admitted.

The sound of her Spanish accent turned both Ty and Toya on. Toya inserted one finger into Mercedes' asshole as she flicked her tongue quickly on her clit.

Mercedes creamed all over Toya's face. Seeing the freak shit that Toya just did almost made Ty hit his climax. He pulled his dick out of his woman and ordered both ladies to lie down. For the next three hours the trio tried many positions. All rolling off the pills, no one wanted to stop. *Oh my God this is the fucking life,* Ty thought as he watched Mercedes ride his dick.

She lifted her fat ass and plopped it back down with skill.

Slap, Slap, Slap, Slap

The sound of her ass slapping against Ty's balls filled the room. Toya stood on the side of the bed watching as she smoked a blunt. Ty felt like he was about to cum and this time he wasn't holding it.

"Get up Ma," Ty said calmly to Mercedes. As she got up, he called out to Toya, "Come sit on it for Daddy," he said sexily as he stared up at his lady.

Toya already knew what time it was. She could tell by the look in his eyes that it was time for him to finish. She slowly eased down onto his rock-hard dick and then began to ride ferociously. She grabbed Ty's neck and applied pressure as she rode aggressively.

"Mmmmm, ahhh, Daddy I love it!" she moaned loudly. Mercedes kissed Toya's lower back as she rose and fell repeatedly on Ty's dick.

Watching Toya ride wasn't enough for Mercedes; she reached down and began to lick Toya's ass and Ty's balls.

"The fuck," Ty moaned as Mercedes gently sucked on his balls. He grabbed Toya's waist and forcibly stroked. His soon to be wife had not stopped riding him. His blood started to build at the head of his dick. "Ahhhhhh," he moaned as he let his seeds spill into the latex glove.

The party of three were all exhausted. Toya laid next to Ty. Her chest heaved up and down as she tried to catch her breath. Lying next to her was Mercedes who was trying to do the same. Before they knew it, they all had drifted off into sleep as the sun was rising.

Ty was the first up. He could never sleep comfortably in the company of someone new. Ty's mind was so fixated with his crazy ass encounter just hours before that he hadn't even noticed Mercedes get up from the bed. She quickly dressed herself in the outfit that she had on the night prior. Ty stood in front of her in just his boxers. *Ay dios mío, he looks good,* she thought as she put her heels on. Ty placed his finger onto his lips signaling for Mercedes to be quiet because of a sleeping Toya.

"Let me walk you to the door," he whispered.

Ty led the way to the front door, she closely followed. He opened the door for her and handed her seven crisp one hundred-dollar bills. Mercedes was no prostitute, but she wasn't going to deny the money given to her.

"Thanks for a good time," he said.

"No Papá, thank ju. If ju ever come to Puerto Rico again, come see me," she said in her heavy accent as she kissed Ty's cheek.

"I'll make sure we do that," Ty said as he watched Mercedes walk to the elevator.

"Even if it's only ju," Mercedes said with a smirk as she winked just before she entered the elevator and disappeared out of his life.

Chapter 11

Since they had been back from Puerto Rico, Ty and Toya's relationship blossomed tremendously. It was like their little getaway brought the spark back into their dying love. Ty fell back from his street life but was still very active in his business while still giving his woman the love and attention that she needed.

Ty walked into his home to find Toya sitting Indian style in the middle of the living room floor. Magazines were scattered about covering the space around her. Names like Vogue, Martha Stewart, and Vera Wang dressed the plush ivory carpet beneath her. "What the hell are you doing, Ma?" Ty asked with a smirk on his face as he watched his bride-to-be make collages on the floor.

"Wedding planning babe. Duh..." she answered without even looking up from her project.

"Hey Ty," a woman said cheerfully as she entered the living room from the kitchen. She carried two sodas and balanced a bowl full of chips in the crease of her arm. Her thick, beige colored thighs rubbed together as she walked towards the couch. The woman was about 5'5 with long, bone straight, jet-black, silky hair that ended just above her ass.

Her chink eyes and chubby cheeks made her resemble a Buddha statue. Her small A-cup breast and small waist only made her hips and thighs look bigger. Ty stared at the girl for a while.

"Babe, you remember Asia, right? She's Pop's girlfriend," Toya said as she flipped through the catalogs.

"Yea, I remember her. I'm gonna leave y'all alone to do this girly shit," Ty said as he leaned down and kissed the top of Toya's forehead before making his exit for the bedroom.

Secretly, Ty didn't like any of the girls that Pop kept as company. They all insisted on living in the fast life that the men had worked in. The only reason he kept his harbored thoughts to himself was because this was the first time in a while that he saw the love of his life happy. She came back from her trip and started going out more and making new friends. She started to live a little and not just have her entire existence revolve around Ty.

The last time Ty felt this negative about a friend Toya had, was way back when she had a high school best friend. Since Toya had lost her best friend all those years ago, Ty remained quiet. Any friend of Toya's that kept her happy was someone he was just going to have to get used to. He made sure to keep his eyes open around the girl though. Trust with him wasn't so easily achieved like how it was with Toya.

"Now that he's out of here, what's the update on his birthday party?" Asia whispered through her full, pink lips.

Asia was twenty-one, African American and Asian, and lived for the street thrill. At the young age of seven, her parents moved their family to the states. Her fourteen years on U.S. soil urbanized her completely. Her accent during conversation peaked rarely. She had met and fell in love with Pop when she was in high school. His hood swagger drove her ass crazy.

He was the street life high that she had been chasing almost all her life. Toya looked around to make sure the coast was clear before she lifted one of her wedding books from the floor. Underneath was a folder with party itinerary in it. Toya had been secretly planning Ty's twenty-seventh birthday bash for the past two months and now August was here.

The plans were set to be pursued in a week's time for a party on a yacht that would circle The Statue of Liberty. With the help of Pop and Bleek, Toya was able to invite all the other members of their crew as well as their associates. The only headache Toya would have would be trying to convince Ty to get dressed up and go out next Saturday. Toya shuffled through the papers showing Asia pictures of the boat and the décor.

She held no expense when it came to her man's birthday. She hired the best party planner that the city had to offer.

"Oooh girl, this shit is fire," Asia said as she filled her mouth with chips.

"Yea, I think out of all of his gifts that he's going to like this one best," Toya said as she held up a picture of a diamond chain. The Cuban links held a diamond-encrusted medallion. It was a white-gold piece of Jesus on a cross. Toya beamed with pride at her selection of a gift, knowing that Ty would love it.

"Alright y'all, I'm out," Ty said as he breezed past the ladies.

Toya jumped at the sound of his voice, and she quickly covered the papers with wedding magazines. "Uh, okay, baby be safe and see you later," Toya yelled out to the back of his head. Ty stood outside in the hallway for a hot minute before he made his way towards the elevator. A smile spread widely across his face. *How can she still not know that I know what she's planning?* he thought as he twirled his car keys in his hand.

A slight chuckle escaped his lips as he thought of the many times in the last two months that Toya had slipped up with her secret birthday plans. Ty had spent an entire month outside of the streets. If it wasn't for a meeting, Bleek handled all transactions for him. He had to admit to himself that being stepped away from the game was a feeling of relief.

He was able to enjoy the Fourth of July with just his lady but today he had to get back to business officially. Today was the day that he had to put his presence back into the streets. He had a meeting set to provide an enormous amount of coke to a new and upcoming crew that was taking the streets by storm. Deals like this called for the boss to show face so, he emerged from his hibernation. He silently prayed that with his appearance back into the hood he still would be able to continue to keep his queen satisfied.

$$$

The dimly lit warehouse in Williamsburg held a cold chill. It was always an eerie feeling that loomed in the air when it came time to meet new niggahs. Seven out of the nine bosses from BS9 sat comfortably at the long, oversized table that stood in the middle of the warehouse under an industrial light.

Of course, Ty and Bleek had to make their grand entrance. Five young men stood idly on the sidelines. They held up the wall as they waited for the meeting to start.

"Yo, y'all come over here. Let me introduce y'all to the team," Pop said in a friendly manner. The five men slowly walked into the light and towards the table to all grab seats.

"This right here is my man Tone." A slim, dark-skinned man with broad shoulders took his seat while nodding his head to greet everyone else.

Pop moved onto the next man beside him. "This right here is my homeboy Rowdy." A thin framed, caramel-colored man with braids quietly greeted the men as he took his seat. Pop then snapped his fingers and pointed to the next man.

"This here… this here…" Pop stopped talking as he rubbed his chin and then continued, "this right here is my bro Stacks."

The tall man with a fresh haircut showed off his chipped tooth as he smirked at his homie's sense of humor. Stacks and Pop went way back, they attended the same public schools together.

"Alright y'all, and these two are the twins, Los and Law," Pop said while pointing at the last two outsiders before he took his own seat.

The twins were indeed identical, their dark skin and same frame was a mirrored image.

"Alright, y'all niggahs done with introductions?" Ty asked as he and Bleek entered the warehouse.

Ty stepped into a room filled with twelve men and his presence was the most felt. His designer royal blue Maison Margiela sneakers tapped powerfully across the concrete floors. Bleek followed closely behind his brother, his walk was just as commanding.

Both men took their seats at the head of the table. Once seated comfortably Ty spoke, "Let's get to it."

"Okay, so Pop brought y'all to my attention. What y'all tryna do here today?" Ty asked as he sat back in his chair and played with his pinky ring. Tone lifted his snapback off his head slightly as he clasped his hands together on top of the table's top.

"We tryna cop some work from you, three keys to be exact. Not on consignment either, I'm talking straight cash," he said calmly.

The members of BS9 eyebrows rose at the notion. Even Ty was taken back at how much the young man before him was asking for.

"Three keys? Straight cash?" Ty question as he continued, "Sheeeeeeesh, that's a lot. Are your pockets that deep?"

Tone chuckled at the doubt in Ty's voice. He stretched in his chair and then spoke.

"Don't worry about my pockets. What's my damage?"

Ty smirked. It was something about the young man in front of him that he had to respect. In a way, he reminded him of himself when he was younger. The rest of the men in the room looked at how the conversation in front of them was playing out. Ty sucked his teeth like food was stuck in them.

"That's nine fifteen with five percent extra added on for travel."

Everyone in the room turned their attention back towards Tone. It was obvious that he was starting to break a sweat. *Damn, I can't look like I don't have it,* Tone thought as he fumbled with what to say next. He rubbed his chin and then grinned before he spoke.

"I've seen brighter days."

"You shouldn't be so stubborn when you're trying to cut a deal." Ty's smile made everyone in the room feel at ease. That was until it quickly faded. "Now let's talk business like grown men."

For the next ten minutes, the men went back and forth on a set price.

"Nine straight, off the boat, no traveler's fee and it's none of that stepped on shit. You don't do business with nobody else but me. This price will remain the same if you only come to me." Ty looked Tone dead in the eyes as he continued to speak, "If I find that you went to anybody else besides me, then I'm shutting your shit down."

Tone listened to every word before he responded.

"Not stepped on huh? We'll leave that up to the fiends."

Tone's manner was flat. He meant exactly what he just said. The aura in the room seemed tense now; both men were so much alike, and everyone seated at the table felt it. Ty smirked mischievously at the younger hustler in front of him.

"Man, this shit is so pure that you could cut the shit twice and it'll still have you drooling."

Everyone in the room laughed at Ty's joke, and the uptight vibe quickly vanished.

"Now that the business part is over," Ty started as he began to get up from his seat, "if Pop didn't already invite y'all niggahs. Next Saturday, I want to invite y'all to my birthday party. It's on a boat too, so make sure y'all—"

"Na niggah! Na… how you found out about this?" Pop asked, cutting Ty off as he laughed. He was completely shocked. He thought these past weeks that he did a good job at hiding the event from him.

"Bleek, you had to tell him bro," Pop said.

Bleek tossed his hands in the air and poked his bottom lip out.

"Nope, deff didn't, now you—"

"Come on P, I know everything," Ty cut Bleek off as he chuckled.

Getting back to what he was saying to begin with, Ty continued.

"Anyways, my lady working hard on this so make sure y'all dress appropriately."

Ty circled the table to dap goodbye to every man in attendance.

"Yo Tone, walk me out," Ty called out as he walked towards the exit. Tone stood from the table and walked over towards the exit confidently.

"What's up?" Tone asked once they were in earshot of just them two.

"I don't know what it is about you scrap, but you remind me of a younger version of myself. Listen, normally when I'm not available I send niggahs to re-up with Bleek."

Tone listened cautiously. Ty continued, "I'm gonna give you this number for me. I want you to always come to me. When you head back to the table Bleek should have the work in a duffle bag for y'all."

Ty gave Tone the number and then the two men dapped one another in farewell. Ty had to privately admit that he was impressed with the young man. At only the age of twenty-two, Tone and his men parted with almost a million dollars like it was nothing. Future endeavors would hopefully prove that all the men could do beneficial work together.

Chapter 12

Saturday night came quick. Toya stood at the foot of the bed and gently applied cocoa butter to her body. Her mind was running a mile a minute as she thought of ways to get Ty out of the bed. Ty lay sprawled out in the middle of the bed in front of her with his basketball shorts on and nothing else.

"Come on boo, get your ass in the shower; we got to go," Toya whined as she kicked the end of the bed.

"Come on Ma, get back in the bed," Ty said groggily as he patted the vacant spot beside him.

"Hell no! Noooo way!" Toya sashayed in her towel to the bed and began to pull Ty out of it.

"Let's go! Dinner on this boat is romantic and we're doing it!"

Ty finally decided to get out of the bed. Sweat beads formed onto Toya's forehead from trying to get the birthday boy up and active. *Alright, let me stop giving her such a hard time,* he thought as he smiled before he pulled Toya closer to him. He kissed her lips gently and then made his way towards their master bathroom.

As soon as Ty closed the bathroom door behind him, she rushed to the French imported chest in their room and pulled open the bottom drawer. Inside was a black velvet box. The chain she bought for his birthday had just been completed the day before. She placed the jewelry box onto the bed that she had just made and then made her way to her vanity to put her face on for the night.

The vast rollers wrapped in her hair were slowly plummeting. She had been prepped and almost ready to go for going on three hours, but of course she was waiting on Ty. She looked in the mirror at her reflection and noticed something that she hadn't in years. She saw pure happiness. In the past week she had seen a little less of Ty but, yet and still she was still fulfilled.

Her buzzing cellphone drew her attention.

"Hello?" she answered.

"Like… where are you guys?" Loud music could be heard in the background, but Toya still knew Asia's voice.

"Girl it's like this niggah is dragging his feet on purpose or some shit—"

Toya stopped talking immediately once she heard the bathroom door open.

She was so busy trying to hear what Asia was saying that she didn't even notice the shower water shut off. She quickly ended her call and placed her phone onto her vanity.

"Who were you talking to?" Ty asked with a raised eyebrow. Toya turned around quickly to find him standing before her completely naked with his towel in his hand. He was drying off his curly fro. Her eyes immediately gravitated towards his private area.

"Um, nobody," she said as she gulped hard, nervously.

He smiled sinisterly as he walked towards her; his hard print bopped alongside his thigh with each stride.

"Uh uh, Tyshawn, back away from me." Toya laughed as she placed her arms far out in front of her to try and stop his approach.

"Real quick," he said as he began to kiss her neck. Instantly the space between her thighs became moist. She almost gave in to temptation until she looked at the clock on the nightstand.

The time read 9:50 p.m. and they had to be at the dock by eleven.

"No baby, we can't. We have to be at dinner by eleven before the ship takes off."

Ty pouted his bottom lip out but understood. The last thing he wanted was to mess up everything that Toya had been planning. He walked over to the nightstand to grab his lotion and deodorant when a box on the bed grabbed his attention.

Toya watched him through the mirror that she was doing her makeup in. He picked up the box and opened it with a huge grin spread on his face.

"Damn Ma, this shit is so icy," he said as he held the medallion in his hand.

"This me?" he asked as he placed the chain around his neck. The medallion fell to the middle of his chest. "Oh yea! Now I'm in the birthday spirit. Thank you, baby girl," he said cheerfully as he made his way to his walk-in closet.

After Toya finished her makeup, she made her way to her walk-in closet. The couple had so many clothes that most of the designer gear that hung on the hangers and racks still had tags on them. They had less than an hour to be fully dressed and out of the door.

$$$

By 10:50 sharp the couple was walking down the border to board the yacht. The two-level, ivory-colored boat stood tall in the waters. A gentleman at the entry, the boarding attendant, looked at Toya and spoke, "It's very nice to see you again Mrs. Barnett, and this must be Mr. Barnett. Follow me and I will show you where you will be seated."

Ty and Toya wore matching Christian Louboutin shoes. It's like their minds were on the same brain wave when they were getting dressed separately in their closets. They both were wearing all white from head to toe. Toya's Saint Laurent pants suit hugged her body. Her blazer was buttoned in the middle and underneath she wore only a lace bra.

Her Double D's sat at attention. Her hair held loose curls and her makeup was done flawlessly. Ty's Tom Ford suit was tailored perfectly for his frame. *I finally got somewhere to wear this shit,* Ty thought to himself as he fixed his diamond-studded cufflinks. His shape up with a side part was sharp. He rubbed his fingers through his soft curly fro before the attendant opened the doors to a room that held one hundred fifty people.

"SURPRISE," everyone in the room yelled out loudly. Music started to play. Ty looked around and had to admit that his lady did the damn thing. White balloons and décor filled the room. Five different photographers circled the room to take pictures of the entire party. The first people to come up and dap Ty were his team. Toya kissed Ty gently on the lips and then walked off to go and find Asia, leaving him to catch up with all his many guests.

Ty looked around at his homeboys and was filled with pride. Every single last one of the other eight bosses were all dressed to perfection with a date on their arm. Bleek walked up to Ty with a bottle of champagne in his hand.

"What up boy boy!" Bleek said excitedly. "It's your day my niggah!"

Ty took the bottle of champagne from Bleek and then popped the cork. Bubbles erupted from the nose of the bottle and fell onto the hardwood floor. Almost immediately an employee dressed in a suit cleaned up the mess.

"To getting money and to family," Ty yelled as he held the bottle in the air for a toast.

"To getting money and to family," the team said in unison as they lifted their own personal bottles.

The party had exquisite food and endless amount of drinks available to all in attendance. Ty worked the room confidently. Everyone knew that he was a self-made boss. Besides his heavy clout in the streets, you could tell just by how he carried himself.

The party had been circling the Hudson River for the past two hours and still he did not greet all his guests. The room Toya booked for this function was filled.

"What up playboy?" someone called out to the birthday boy. Ty turned around to see Tone and his team. They embraced one another. Ty was impressed; the same men he had seen a few days prior dressed in hood gear cleaned up very nicely.

Just like his team, the team standing in front of him all had dates on their arms. Ty took note.

There were two types of hood niggahs: One that will be nothing but a hood niggah because they don't know anything else, and then you have a hood niggah that can transform. He could tell that the men in front of him were the same as he. They were all hood niggahs that wouldn't be hood niggahs forever.

"How you tell us so much about wifey working hard at this party but she ain't here?" Tone asked as he pulled the woman on his arm closer.

Ty couldn't help but to notice how beautiful the girl on Tone's arm was. She was a slim chick with high cheekbones and doe-like eyes. Her full lips curved at the corners when she smiled. Her long, dark hair was pressed straight. She looked like a real-life Pocahontas and Ty was infatuated. He broke from his trance to respond.

"Na, her crazy ass around here somewhere. She gone make her presence known sooner or later—"

The music stopped playing as someone began to speak over the microphone.

"Hey everybody, I want to take this time to thank everyone for coming out tonight."

"There she goes," Ty whispered to Tone.

He then made his way towards his lady as she continued to talk. Tone stared at Toya as she spoke and was struck. Her mahogany skin looked smooth to the touch. Her pearly white teeth clinked together when she said certain words.

Maleeka, Tone's date, saw where his attention went.

"Ah hem," she said quietly as she nudged him in his rib cage. Tone parted from his trance as he gently squeezed her hand, letting her know she had nothing to worry about.

"It's time to cut this cake. I know you hate cake Babe, but… oh well."

Toya shrugged her shoulders and everyone in the room laughed at her officiousness. An employee dressed in a black and white suit wheeled out a two-tier cake.

The Las Vegas themed cake had slot machines and poker chips scattered about. The gathering all sang "Happy Birthday" in unison. Ty looked around at all his guests and just smiled. His woman stood on the side of him and sang loudly as she clapped her hands. Once everyone stopped wishing Ty a happy birthday, the DJ dropped a track that everyone knew.

Lamborghini Mercy
Your chick she so thirsty
I'm in that two seat Lambo
With your girl she tryna jerk me

Men and women danced together. Toya popped her ass on her man to the beat. Asia drunkenly stumbled around the dance floor looking for Pop. At her young age, Asia still had not yet mastered the art of the *pretty girl sip* or other known as, drinking until you felt nice and not until you were drunk.

The DJ switched over to a reggae tune. Mr. Vegas' song that was just released "Bruk It Down" vibrated the walls of the decorated conference room. Asia began to tick her wide hips in the middle of the dance floor. One of the plus ones found himself a comfortable spot right behind Asia's ass, and she grinded hard on her new dance partner.

A crowd slowly formed around the dancing couple. The man placed his hands around Asia's small waist to pull her closer. Bleek was listening to Pop talk, but his attention was completely over his younger protégé's shoulder.

"Hello niggah!" Pop said as he snapped his fingers in Bleek's face and continued to talk, "You don't hear me talking to you, bro?"

Bleek said nothing and just simply grabbed Pop by his shoulders and turned him around. Pop looked through the crowd and saw his woman grinding her ass on a stranger. His ears rung and sweat began to form on his forehead almost instantly.

"Yo, Pop chill." Before Bleek could continue, Pop stormed off towards the crowd. He pushed guests out of his way forcibly. Ty stopped enjoying his dance from his wifey once he saw the scene that was about to unfold.

He stepped away from Toya and walked swiftly towards the crowd. *Shit!* Toya thought as she watched her drunk friend shake her ass. She jogged lightly through the crowd. She wanted badly to reach her friend before Pop did. Unfortunately, she was too late. Pop yoked Asia up by her satin halter-top.

"What the fuck!" she yelled drunkenly. Asia looked Pop in the eyes and saw a man that she didn't recognize.

Pop's pride had him furious. Everyone at this party saw his woman shaking and ticking her rear end on the next man.

"Yo! My man, you don't think you doing too—" Before Asia's former dance partner could even get anything else out, he was dropped by the forceful blow to the mouth.

Pop shook the pain out of his hand as he yoked Asia back up with his free hand.

"Who fucking mans is this?" Pop shouted.

He wanted to kick who ever brought the niggah along ass too. Ty tried to grab Pop, but it was no use; he was beyond livid.

"Get the fuck off of me Ty," Pop said sternly as spit foamed at the corners of his mouth.

Toya tried to rush in between Asia and Pop, but Ty held her back.

"Mind your business Ma. I would hate to have to kill my little bro if he puts a hand on you by mistake," Ty whispered in her ear as he held her tightly.

"Pop, you're hurting me," Asia cried out. "Can someone move this niggah off me?" she screamed.

Tears rolled continuously down her cheeks, but no one interfered. Pop mushed Asia out of the crowd.

"Go clean the fuck up! I can't take yo' ass nowhere," he shouted as he walked away from the crowd in the opposite direction from which he had just pushed Asia.

"We are now arriving back at the dock. Thank you for sailing with Seas of the Day," an employee spoke over the loudspeaker.

Toya squirmed from Ty's grip, she then ran towards the bathrooms to check on Asia. *These niggahs are wild,* Tone thought as he ushered his crew and his lady towards the exit. Toya busted into the bathroom to find Asia face down in a line of coke. A weary feeling washed over Toya. She felt sick to her stomach.

"What the fuck are you doing?" she yelled.

Asia held her head back as she let the euphoria aid her pain. She wiped her nose in the mirror and checked for any traces of residue. It was as if she didn't even hear the person talking to her. Toya closed the bathroom door behind her and pushed Asia into the stall.

"I said what the fuck are you doing?" she asked again.

"What the fuck does it look like? What, you came in here to yoke me the fuck up like how Pop just did?" Asia asked honestly as she sniffled, waiting on an answer.

Toya's eyes shifted from the fish scale on the bathroom sink to Asia. She washed the remaining lines down the drain.

"Īkagen'ni shite. What ah you doing?" Asia asked as she tried to fight her way to the drugs that Toya was washing down the sink. Her Japanese language surfaced because of her anger. Knowing that Toya had no idea what she had just said, she repeated herself in English.

"Come onnnnn."

Toya pushed her back into the stall as she spoke.

"Come on nothing! How long have you been doing this shit?" She was disgusted.

"What the fuck does it matter T? It helps with a lot of pain that I deal with; it makes me forget yo."

Asia cried hysterically, her makeup ran down her face. Toya looked at the girl in front of her and started to feel bad. *What kind of demons is this girl battling to resort to this?* she thought as she hugged her friend.

A knock on the door interrupted the two women from their sentimental moment.

"Ma, it's time to go," Ty could be heard on the other side of the door.

"I'm coming," Toya called out.

"Listen, does Pop know about this?" she whispered to Asia. She didn't even have to answer the question. The tears that welled up in her lids told Toya that this was now their little secret.

"I'm gonna try and help you but you need to ease up on this shit yo! It could really kill you," Toya whispered as she pushed the hair out of Asia's face.

"I'll call you okay," she added.

Toya opened the door to the bathroom to see both Ty and Pop standing on the other end.

"I love you Toya," Asia whispered once she saw the look that Pop gave her.

"I love you too little sister." Toya walked away hand in hand with Ty. She couldn't shake the feeling in the pit of her stomach. She couldn't believe that she just witnessed her only friend doing drugs in front of her.

"Is everything good with her?" Ty asked.

"Yea, she's good," Toya lied.

Chapter 13

2 months later

The autumn leaves crinkled beneath Toya's feet as she rushed home. The cool breeze from the October air pushed its way through Toya's leather jacket. Ty had been blowing up her phone for the past hour, but she kindly kept shooting him to her voicemail. Businesses decorated their store's front with leaves and pumpkins. Halloween was just a week away. Toya dreadfully hated holidays like Halloween. To her, it was just a constant reminder that she had yet to have the kid that she'd been begging for. She slowed down her strut to get her vibrating phone out of her pocket.

"Fuck out of here," she mumbled to herself as she sent Ty's twentieth call to voicemail.

In the past two months, Ty had been once again involved heavily in the streets and seemed to have forgotten where home was. Like promised, Toya started spending more time with Asia to help her with her slow growing addiction. She tried to drill in her friend's head that any addiction could be stopped at the drop of a hat. "It's not that easy T," Asia would always say to her. Toya felt as if her being around was becoming effective. What she didn't know was that when she went home to Ty, Asia snorted more lines than she could count.

Toya finally reached home to find that the chain was on the house door. *Now this niggah decides to come home?* she thought as she closed the door shut and then began to bang on it. When there was no answer, she pulled her iPhone out of her pocket and called Ty, only to be sent to voicemail.

"I know you hear me banging on this fucking door Tyshawn!"

Toya was livid. She turned her back to face the door and slowly kicked the steel frame. Once she heard locks turning, she stopped.

"Must you be so fucking dramatic?" he asked serenely. "Now where the fuck was you that you couldn't answer your phone?"

Toya completely ignored Ty's question as she made her way towards the bedroom.

"The fuck? You don't hear me talking to you?"

Ty was starting to get furious. "HELLO!" he yelled.

The bass from his rumble shook the walls. He hated being ignored and he hated repeating himself; these were all things that Toya knew. In a real nonchalant manner, Toya finally spoke.

"When you're out handling business, you can't seem to answer your phone. So, I decided to not answer mine. What's the problem?"

Toya started to undress as if their conversation wasn't even happening.

"I'm not fucking playing with you Latoya. Don't let your petty shit get you fucked up in here."

Ty's tone was severe. Deciding on not to further ignite the massive flame at hand, Toya just answered honestly, "I was in Park Slope at Asia's house."

Ty inwardly cringed at her statement. He couldn't stand Asia's ass.

Lately, Pop had been confiding in Ty. He expressed that he thought Asia was acting weird towards him. He knew something was irregular with her.

"So, you go over there and suddenly come up with the notion that you don't have a phone? Huh?" he asked curiously. Toya continued undressing and then walked towards the bathroom to wash.

"I am talking to you!" Ty couldn't understand why Toya was behaving in this manner.

He grabbed her arm firmly and turned her towards him. Since walking in the door, she hadn't looked him in the eyes. When turned to face him, Toya couldn't hide her deepest secret. He stared her in the face for a long moment. Her gaze shifted rapidly. It was like she couldn't look him directly in the eyes.

"Why can't you look at me? What are you not telling me?" he asked desperately.

His brows dipped in sorrow. "Since when do you keep things from me?"

That was what broke Toya's emotional barrier. Her eyes watered quickly and soon tears sashayed down her cheeks. *What am I doing to my relationship?* she asked herself as she peered into the windows of Ty's soul.

She knew that if she fessed up, Ty would be beyond irate. Not only was she keeping secrets from him, but she was beginning to treat him differently. "I…" Her words got caught in her throat.

"I have been keeping something from you."

Lines of distress formed on Ty's forehead as he let go of her arm. He wiped his strong hand over his face. A million thoughts swam in his mind. *Keeping something from me? What the fuck would she not tell me?*

Toya stood uselessly on the sidelines and watched as Ty went through his motions. *Is she cheating on me? I'm gone kill that niggah. I'm gone kill her ass.* Ty felt sick to his stomach. He held onto the bed's post for support.

"Just say it," his words cracked in his throat.

Toya began to cry instantly. The secret wasn't even hers to tell but she knew that she had to spill the beans to save her relationship. She controlled her breathing. If she was going to come clean, she had to just say everything at once.

"I've been spending time by Asia's so much because you're never here. I hate being home. I hate being alone."

She paused to try and think of where to go next. *She hates being alone? This sounds like a cheating confession intro.* Ty let his inner thoughts roam freely. He began to get angry at the thought of another man not even touching but just being in her presence. As territorial as it may sound, she was his. He had put his stamp on her years ago and his ink of possession was permanent. He wouldn't hesitate to exterminate another man for simply breathing the same air as her.

"First of all, that shit about you being alone because I'm out making money is fucking old now, okay. You don't complain when you're spending the shit. So, I'm done hearing about it!" Ty realized that he was shouting so he lowered his tone.

"Latoya… before my mind goes elsewhere… say what you have to say."

"Asia's doing coke."

The statement came out clear and almost echoed throughout their apartment.

"WHAT?" Ty rushed Toya, grabbing her by her esophagus in the process.

"You on that shit too huh? That's why you been acting different," his bark terrified the neighbors.

"No baby, I swear," Toya cried helplessly.

"I just promised her that I wouldn't tell anyone."

Ty let go of his lover's throat. Toya winced in pain as she touched her aching neck. Her tears were now endless.

"How are you loyal to that bitch and not your man? You've been keeping this secret from me for how long?"

Ty paced the floor in front of her as he spoke. He had to keep his legs moving to keep his hands to himself. Hearing stillness for too long he screamed, "HOW LONG?"

"Since your birthday," she said inaudibly as she lowered her head.

"Two fucking months," he scoffed. "You gotta be shitting me right now. You can't be trusted."

Ty began to gather his keys and wallet to make his exit.

"Baby no, please, don't go!"

Toya cried out as she followed closely behind Ty. She pulled on his t-shirt as an attempt to stop him in his tracks.

"Get the fuck off of me Latoya."

Ty spun around with his hand raised. He had half the mind to slap the taste of out her mouth, but the look of fear plastered on her face was what stopped him. He was no woman beater and he wasn't about to let his emotions change that.

He rubbed his hands through his curly mane as stress washed over him.

"Do you know just how dangerous it is for an addict to be around a fucking drug dealer?"

Ty's question lingered in the air. He knew exactly how difficult it was. He had to cut ties with his own mother because of her addiction. The strain of love in between those white lines were so bad that he didn't know if his mother had found help or if she was toe tagged somewhere, and he honestly didn't care.

His heart began to feel for Pop.

"Do you know how much that little niggah loves that bitch?"

All the questions he was asking were all rhetorical. "When he finds out, this shit will fucking break him! Do you hear me?"

The longer Ty spoke the louder his voice became.

"You fucking let someone else put all their trust in you to the point where you jeopardized your fucking relationship. You couldn't trust me enough to tell me? You didn't think that we could have tried to help that girl? There are places where addicts can receive help Latoya." He spoke his sentences clearly and emphasized on every word. Toya listened thoroughly and just cried. "ANSWER ME!" The bass from his voice caused her body to shake.

"Of course, I trusted you. I… trust… you," she said through sobs.

"Na, you don't, and the only reason why I think you didn't say anything is because you probably on that shit yourself."

Ty walked towards the front door. He looked back at the love of his life. Even soaked in tears her image was still breathtaking. Her natural glow still illuminated through the snotty nose and swollen bloodshot eyes.

"Since you want to lie like the rest of these bitches, I'm gone start to treat you like them. Birds of a feather flock together Ma." That was the last thing he said before he slammed the front door behind him.

$$$

Ty needed air, he needed time to sort out all this new-found information that he had just received.

"Yo, Pop call me when you get this. It's urgent."

Ty left a message on Pop's voicemail. There was no way he was going to let his young homie be in the dark about this any longer. Ty sat in his parked car and just held his vibrating phone in his hand. Toya kept calling. *What the fuck doesn't she get? I just need space,* he thought as he pulled his car out of the parking garage.

He skillfully sped his white 2012 Lexus is300 over lanes on the northbound FDR drive. Since Pop wasn't available for a talk that was necessary, Ty had to be around his right-hand man. Within the next half hour Ty was pulling up to Bleek's building. The feel in the boogie down Bronx was a different vibe than Brooklyn's.

Ty never understood why Bleek had decided to move so far out being from Bushwick. Bleek made money just how Ty did but he lived simply. He had lived in this same one-bedroom apartment since the brotherhood were youngsters. While walking up to the building, Ty saw an older woman carrying bags over the threshold.

"Hold the door please," Ty called out as he lightly jogged towards the entryway.

"You need help Miss?" he asked as he looked down at the many bags that the woman was carrying.

"I don't want to be a bother, it's okay hunn—"

"That's nonsense," Ty cut her off and then continued, "I'm going to the top floor anyways. I can help."

Ty wrapped all six bags around his fingers and then ascended the steps behind the woman. She looked to be at least sixty. Her strut up the stairs let Ty know that even in her rising age she still had spunk. They engaged in small talk as they climbed to the third floor, her destination.

"You're a blessing baby. Any woman would be blessed to have you," the old woman thanked as she began to dig into her change purse.

"No, no," Ty stopped her, "it's not needed."

He smiled as he walked up the last flight to Bleek's crib.

$$$

Bleek sat relaxed on his sofa as he played his favorite game, *Call of Duty: Black Ops II*. His two guests engaged in small talk as they watched the television. A knock at the door broke him from his concentration. *Who the fuck is that?* he thought as he stood from his sofa to go and answer his door.

"What up boy boy?" Bleek said as he embraced his big brother. "What brings you through?"

Ty followed Bleek towards the living room. "Mad shit bro. Wifey gone make me—" Ty stopped speaking once he realized two other bodies were in the living room.

"Why you ain't say you had company when we were at the door?" Ty whispered to Bleek.

"This ain't company," Bleek whispered back.

Bleek pointed to the couch, directing Ty to take a seat.

"Bro you already know baby girl, Eternity. This is her little sister, Tori."

Ty looked over, gave Eternity a head nod and then stopped once he looked at Tori. His breath caught in his throat. The light-skinned beauty sat across from her older sister at the dining room table.

Ty looked through the glass table at her thighs. The denim fabric that covered them hugged her thickness. Her fat cheeks rose, and her small eyes squinted as she gave a warm smile. Her pink lips parted showing off her trained, straight white fangs. Her thick locks were pulled up into a high bun. Her natural, earthy beauty was stunning. Her aura was even beautiful. I'm talking the rainbow after a summer sun shower, beautiful.

"Uhh bro… what was you saying about sis?" Bleek interrupted Ty's trance when he passed his boy an extra Xbox 360 controller.

Ty didn't know why, but he felt completely comfortable in front of this new company. He spoke freely. He explained everything to Bleek, sparing no detail.

"So, you think she's using?" Bleek asked.

"Honestly, she hasn't given me a reason to truly believe that, but I would be a liar if I told you that I could just go back to trusting her."

Ty pushed down hard on the controller's buttons as he answered.

Always being one to be outspoken, Eternity added her two cents into the conversation.

"I honestly think that she's not. If she was, she wouldn't have ratted her girl out that easily. It would have been like she was tryna hide her secret too. I know crackheads and shit, they would deny, deny, deny to family when it comes to their problem."

Ty paused the game and then turned around to give the woman talking his attention. *Who the fuck asked her?* he thought, but then he had to admit privately, *she got a good point.*

"Whether she's using or not it doesn't fucking matter, she's still a liar."

Ty pressed play to continue playing the game.

"See, that's the problem. Niggahs take situations like this and still find negativity no matter how bad the situation could have been. Ohhhhh, just slit her at the throat why don't you because she wants to be loyal to her friend too. Y'all niggahs make me sick." The sweet melody of Tori's voice drew Ty's attention.

Her sarcasm was something rare to him. Other females wouldn't even dare to be sarcastic with him. Knowing who he was, no one dared. But this one, this girl right here didn't care who he was, her mouth curved for no one.

"Oh? Is that right?" he asked as he raised an eyebrow and smirked.

Tori took the lit blunt from her sister and then deeply inhaled. She sensually blew a curve of smoke out her mouth. The stare down she was having with Ty was an intense one. "Damn right," she said and then smiled.

Chapter 14

Later that night…

The sun faded in the sky as the night began to call. The party of four all smoked and played the game together. Bleek and Eternity branched off into his bedroom, leaving the couple alone in the living room. Hours had passed and Ty had forgotten why he was so mad in the first place.

He needed this, a night with no drama. Ty laughed as he listened to Tori tell one of her many stories about growing up with her sister. He enjoyed watching her smile. The way little crinkles formed at the corner of her eyes could make the toughest man smirk.

"Go ahead." Tori paused as she took a pull from the rotating blunt before passing it back to Ty.

"Tell me some shit about you and Bleek growing up; he said y'all went way back."

Ty grabbed the neatly wrapped cannabis from Tori's manicured fingertips. Her sun kissed, yellow-colored nails touched his fingers and did something to him. In the moment of passing their drug of choice, their eyes drew into one another. *Why is he looking at me like this?* Tori thought quietly as she smiled slightly. "You're a pretty girl Ma," Ty said coolly.

His bloodshot eyes held a tint of gloss over them from his fucked up state. Instantly, Tori blushed.

"Thank you," she replied bashfully as she moved a piece of loose hair from in front of her face nervously. Ty yawned and stretched his arms out. He was tired of playing the game, so he placed the controller beside him.

It was getting late. He checked his phone and saw that the time had passed him tremendously. It was three in the morning and he had over twenty missed calls from Toya. Looking at the missed calls pissed him off all over again. He sighed deeply as he placed his phone back into his pocket.

Tori stood from the black couch and walked over to the entertainment center. Ty couldn't help but to notice her switch. It was natural. She didn't try too hard to sway her hips from side to side. She did it effortlessly. Her small waist, bubble butt and thick thighs stretched her jeans to capacity.

She changed the channel so that she could flip through Bleek's music playlist. Silence should have filled the living room until Tori chose a song to play but instead, the sounds of grunts and moans filled the air in the distance. It was obvious what Bleek and Eternity were doing in the room down the hall.

"They can't be dead ass," Ty said as he laughed.

"They really are though," Tori said agreeing.

"Ooooh! This is my song!" She bopped and snapped her fingers to silence until the beat dropped.

Love In Between The White Lines

Right here what we gon' do is go back

Way back

Way back, yeah

I met him when I was a

little girl, he gave me

He gave me poetry

and he was my first

Tori sang along with Erykah Badu's throwback hit.

"What you know about this?" Ty yelled playfully over the blasting music as he bobbed his head to the beat. "Boy bye!" she said as she waved her hand in the air. She sashayed her hips to the beat while taking her hair out of its confinement.

The hair tie rested gently around her wrist as she played in her locks. Her thick brown hair fell at her shoulders. She took her assigned seat right back next to Ty; this time she was a little closer. She threw her leg over his. His heart began to beat quickly, not for what he was feeling but for the wrong he felt he would for sure commit.

She looked him deep in his brown eyes. His strong hand was placed on her upper thigh.

"You tired?" she asked low and sexually.

"Na," he lied as he licked his lips.

"Good… play me in crazy eights," she said cheerfully as she jumped up and began to walk to the dining table.

What! She wants to play cards? Ty laughed hysterically in his head at what he thought was about to go down.

He stood and stretched, an attempt at moving his stiff dick from being noticeable through his G Star army fatigue cargo pants.

"Come on Ma, you're not fucking with me," he said as he took his seat across from her at the dining room table. He noticed how small she was compared to his stature. She had to be about 5'1.

The couple stared at one another as they played. "Damn, you're pretty good at this," he said as he picked up four cards.

"What's the suit now?" he asked.

"Uhhhhh…. I'm gone go with hearts," she said sweetly as she put down a four of hearts.

"Okay, so since I'm about to bust your ass in this last game, what do I get when I win?" Ty asked with a smile as he organized the set of cards in his hand.

"You done? Organizing your hand that is?" she asked.

Ty frowned at how she completely ignored his statement. She came across as slightly rude, but he had leather for skin, so it didn't bother him. He nodded his head that he was finished.

"Okay now… skip you back to me, skip you back to me, and reverse it back to me, last card." Toya dropped an eight of clubs on top of her jack of diamonds. "Out," she said confidently.

"Son, how?" Ty asked out loud as he laughed.

He placed his cards on top of the table to show his shitty hand. Tori looked down and began to laugh.

"You really thought you was gonna beat me with that shit?" she asked before she continued, "Now that I won, you can give me your number."

Her smile was hypnotizing. It was something that he damn sure wasn't gonna say no to.

"Go get your phone," he ordered.

Although Ty should have been feeling some form of guilt, he felt nothing.

"Just friends, right?" he asked as he handed her the phone with his number added into the contacts.

"I know your situation, just friends," she said as she smiled.

He had begun to gather his jacket and make his departure.

"I'm texting you now so you can have the number, *friend*."

Ty smiled at her sense of humor.

"Goodnight," he said just before he closed the front door behind him.

Ty smiled as his phone vibrated in his palm. He skipped two and three steps down the stairs; all he wanted was his bed. He read the message as the morning's mist kissed his face.

"Get home safe 'friend.' Hit me whenever you want to chill or just talk =) <3 - Tori."

The smiley face and heart emoji caused a grin to spread across his face. He sat back in his driver's seat and started his car. Reality started to slowly creep back into his cognizance. *Damn, I still need to deal with this fucking drama,* he thought as he headed home.

By the time Ty reached home, Toya was nestled comfortably inside of the silver, satin-colored sheets of their king-size bed. As he glimpsed at his sleeping beauty, he had begun to feel a little guilt-ridden about having another woman be able to grab his attention. Although his attention was elsewhere for only a moment, he felt like if he still entertained Tori it could cause serious problems later down the line.

Ty didn't even bother to get into the shower; he was exhausted. He peeled the clothes from his body and slowly laid under the comforter. He didn't want to wake Toya at all; he was afraid the sound of her voice would make him angry all over again.

$$\$$$

The aroma of turkey bacon, eggs and French toast woke Ty from his slumber. He took a deep whiff and his stomach began to growl. He rubbed the crust from the corner of his eyes and glanced at the clock on the nightstand. It read 4:17 pm. *Damn, I slept for ten hours.* He yawned and then allowed his toes to hit the plush carpet beneath him.

Toya knew him too well. Ty never ate breakfast at times when it was called for. He always preferred his sunny side up eggs when the sun was damn near close to setting. He followed the sound of sizzling bacon grease. His destination ended at the kitchen. Toya stood with her back facing him.

She hummed along to the sweet melodies of John Legend.

"Baby hmm hmm, hmm hmm we lose control," her soft voice sang lowly.

Ty just stood in the entryway and watched his queen glide across the porcelain floors. She showed how skillful she was in the kitchen. Ty just closed his eyes and said nothing. He was just soaking in the brief moment of peace. With all their bickering lately, a slight moment of stillness was needed.

John Legend sang in his ears, and it relaxed him.

Baby, tonight you need that, tonight believe that
tonight I'll be the best you ever had
I don't want to brag, but I'll be
the best you ever had

Guilt started to simmer over inside of his body. *What the fuck was I thinking last night?* No, Ty did not cheat the night before but to him, he did something way worse. He gave another woman his attention. Toya had heard Ty enter her space moments ago, but she halted her own body from turning to face him every time the thought crossed her mind. *Is he still angry with me?*

She flipped the French toast in the pan as she let her thoughts fill her. Once the last piece of food finished frying in the pan, Toya knew she had to face her demons. She turned around to face Ty, but no one stood there.

Ty stood in the bedroom with his phone in his hand. He didn't know why he had walked away from the kitchen. Deep down inside, he couldn't face Toya. It wasn't because of her actions, he still couldn't see himself trusting her but now he couldn't trust himself.

The ringing phone in his hand interrupted his thoughts; it was Bleek.

"He got locked up FOR WHAT!" Ty's shouting caused Toya to race into the bedroom.

"What happened?" she asked frantically.

Ty ignored her as he walked swiftly around the room to throw on clothes.

"Baby… what happened?" she asked again.

"Pop's in jail," he said flatly.

He brushed past her and stormed out of the door. Toya thought about throwing on clothes and following behind him, but she figured her presence was unwanted.

She sat on the edge of the bed and cried silently. Somehow, she felt like things were her fault. She looked for her phone so that she could call Asia to see what was going on. Toya called Asia's phone six times and each call went unanswered.

"Something must be wrong. Maybe she got locked up too," she mumbled. She tossed on clothes and made her way to Asia's apartment that she shared with Pop.

$$$

"Ma'am, you can't walk past this area; this is an active crime scene." A uniformed police officer stood strong in front of Asia's apartment door.

"Crime scene?" she asked as her eyes began to fill with tears.

"This is my sister's house. What happened?"

The officer wanted badly to ignore Toya, but the sadness that her tone was cloaked in broke him from his daily on the job attitude.

"Oh, okay ma'am, well your sister was involved in a pretty bad domestic. She was sent to New York Methodist over on 6th Ave."

Toya's head spun as she made her way back towards the elevators.

"Thank you," she mouthed to the officer before stepping into the steel box.

The walk to her friend was a quick one. Asia only lived a few blocks from the hospital. Toya rushed through the automatic doors and jogged straight to the emergency room information desk.

"Hi, how may I help you?" a white woman with red hair in a chipper voice asked.

Toya was breathing deeply from her light jog to the hospital.

"I'm here to see my sister. She was rushed in. Her name is Asia Cho."

Toya impatiently waited for the woman to type in the name. Her eyes squinted as she read the computer's screen.

"Here you go dear, take this visitor's pass and you can sit over there and wait. She's in surgery right now but I'm pretty sure that a doctor will be out to update you soon."

The woman's tone was soft as she passed Toya the red pass. Many thoughts burned Toya's brain as she sat in the steel seat. She placed three calls to Ty.

"What the fuck is this niggah doing?" she mumbled to herself as her last call rang and then went to voicemail. She rolled her eyes as she said the statement.

"Is there a family member for an Asia Cho?"

A doctor dressed in blue scrubs called out repeatedly. Toya sat still as she looked at the doctor call again and again. The slim built woman pushed her strands of blonde hair away from her face as she spoke. "That's me," Toya whispered.

"That's me," she said louder.

She stood from her chair and met the doctor halfway in the lobby.

"I'm Toya, her sister. What happened?"

"Hi, my name is Dr. Amanda Peters. Right now, she's still in surgery. When she first came into the E.R she was unconscious. So, we took her to C.T. That is when we discovered that she had a very severe subdural hematoma."

"What is that? A subdural hematoma?" Toya's eyes watered as she asked.

"That's a brain bleed."

Toya covered her mouth as tears began to slide down her flushed cheeks. The doctor's eyebrows curved in sadness as she continued.

"So, she had to be rushed into surgery. I decided that a craniotomy would be our best option. That's a procedure where we remove a piece of her skull to relieve some of the pressure that's on the brain."

The hospital's walls began to spin for Toya.

"So, how is she? Like, like, will she-she be umm, okay after this?" Toya's words skipped as tears threatened to fall again. "Actually, right now, she's still in surgery so we don't—"

"Paging Dr. Peters to E.R seven. Paging Dr. Peters to E.R seven."

The hospital's intercom spoke loudly.

"I'm sorry, I have to go," Dr. Peters said to Toya before she began to walk away.

"I'll be back to update you as soon as I can," she said reassuringly before she disappeared behind the double doors.

Toya slowly dragged her feet back to her station. She placed her head into her hands and rocked her body back and forth. She tried her best to soothe her racing heart.

"What the fuck did he do to her?" she whispered to herself as tears fell onto her lap.

Chapter 15

Ty and Bleek stood quietly outside of the courthouse. They both hated walking in and out of those doors; being on the same block of it made their skin crawl. Bleek broke the silence.

"So, they just gonna deny his bail like that?"

Ty rubbed his hand over his face as he began to walk towards a nearby parking garage.

"Hell yeah, they gone deny his bail. He's being charged with attempted murder and drug possession with the intent to sell. The only thing we can do now is pray her ass don't die and just keep in touch with his lawyer."

"Pop is a baby bro," Bleek said sadly as he pulled the handle to his car door.

"He was still bred for these streets, he got this."

Ty doubted his own words. This wouldn't be just any twenty-five to life for street shit. Every single last one of the men on his team could do a life bid on their heads for some shit that they had signed up for. Street beef was what they all breathed. They were all cut from the same cloth and none of them cowered away from the consequences of their ruthless ways.

What Pop was going through was totally different. This could possibly be twenty-five to life for harming the love of his life. That was a different kind of hurt mentally and physically. That's that kind of can't eat because your stomach is in knots pain. That's the pain that would make you feel sick to your stomach and then make you lose your mind.

The couple rode in silence back to Ty's house.

"Toya!" Ty called out as he and Bleek walked into his home.

"Make sure you got clothes on, Bleek with me."

"What's up Sis," Bleek called out as he took a seat on the sofa.

Ty walked to his bedroom to find that Toya was nowhere to be found.

"The fuck she at?" he asked himself.

He noticed his iPhone lying face down on the dresser. *I'm always leaving this shit somewhere,* he thought as he scrolled through his phone. He saw that he had six missed calls and two voicemails from Toya.

"Yo B, she not even here," Ty said as he took a seat onto the couch.

"She must be checking out Asia," Bleek said as he stuffed his mouth with chips and flipped through the television channels.

Whenever he came over to Ty's house, he always made himself at home. He was the kind of houseguest that made themselves familiar with the kitchen. Ty listened to the voicemails before he decided to call her back.

"I don't see why your stupid ass not answering your got damn—"

Ty cut that voicemail off and played the next. *Fucking girl is crazy,* he thought.

Toya's sobs were the first thing that played in his ear. Immediately his heart began to slowly sink in his chest. She had that kind of effect on him. The mere thought of her crying made his body shudder, so to hear the dreadful noise broke his heart.

"She... she's gone. She died in surgery."

Ty placed his phone onto the couch and just stared at the wall blankly. Bleek was too preoccupied with laughing at reruns of *The Fresh Prince of Bel-Air* to notice Ty's change in mood.

"Yo, this niggah always getting kicked the fuck out," Bleek blurted out loudly as he laughed hysterically.

"Yo bro, remember when you kicked Mickey out the spot like that when we were kids?"

Bleek's eyes watered from his laughter as he thought about the distant memory. When he realized that he was the only one laughing, he looked over to find Ty in a trance.

"Ahh ha, Ahh ha." Bleek's laughter halted. "What's up bro?" he asked with deep concern.

A black hole began to form in the pit of Ty's stomach. His youngest protégé, a young man that he raised and groomed for this game allowed love to be his downfall. Secretly, it frightened him. He loved Toya with everything in him, but reality started to alter the way his mind would normally think. *Sooner or later she might be my downfall as well.*

"Pop's gonna get charged with murder; shorty died in surgery," Ty said with no emotion.

Bleek's mind was officially wrecked.

"Damn," he said lowly, "so what do we do now?"

"It's nothing we can do. Out of respect for him, I'll handle her burial arrangements."

Neither one of them uttered another word. This came with the territory. You get in the game and then you start losing people that's close to you, even yourself.

$$$

Pop sat in his cell with his mind sprinting. His feet couldn't stand still any longer; he had to move them. He stood to pace the concrete floors.

"Fuck," he yelled as he punched the concrete wall. "Inmate, settle down," a C.O. yelled. Blood began to trickle down Pop's bruised knuckles.

"Miller, turn around, you have a visitor."

The guard waited for Pop to turn his back towards the cell's gate so that he could unlock it.

Pop turned around and then placed his hands behind his back. The guard placed cuffs around his wrists tightly. Pop winced at the tight grip. He was ushered through the halls of Riker's Island. Other inmates looked on as he passed.

"I'm gone see you later cutie," one inmate said through his cell as he blew kissy faces at Pop. Becoming immediately offended, Pop responded instantly.

"I don't play that shit niggah! I'll murk yo' ass!"

The guard shoved Pop forward. "Keep it moving inmate." The journey to their destination was a short one. Pop was being placed inside one of the many unoccupied interrogation rooms. Once his handcuffs were off his wrist, he was told to have a seat. Pop sat in the steel chair with his hands placed strongly atop of the steel table.

The door cracked open, grabbing Pop's attention.

"Hello Mr. Daquan Miller, my name is Frank Vasquez, this is my partner James Blackwell—"

Completely annoyed, Pop cut the man off.

"What the fuck do y'all want?"

Vasquez smirked as he took a seat across from the young man.

"I'm a very observant man Mr. Miller." He fixed the cufflinks to his suit as he spoke.

"You're in between a rock and a hard place and I can be your out."

Pop raised his eyebrow as he let the Spanish man in front of him continue.

"Now when I say that I'm observant, I mean that I have been watching not only you but also the company that you keep. Now if my knowledge serves me right, you keep close acquaintances with a Tyshawn Barnett, right?"

Pop kept his game face on. Mentioning the name of his mentor broke no sweat.

"Never heard that name before." Pop's tone was flat.

He stared down Vasquez and his partner. *Fuck these niggahs think I'm a rat or some shit!* Pop's inner thoughts were beginning to infuriate him. He hated being locked down but more than anything, he hated being in front of these two officers.

"Now I think this visit is over. Seems like you donut eating bastards wasted a trip down here."

Pop stood from his seat and then knocked on the steel door, alerting the correctional officer that it was time for him to be escorted back to his cage.

"You know what Pop, we didn't waste a trip. I thought that I would come down here and try and make a deal with you considering that your attempted murder charge just got bumped up to murder in the first degree. But hey, maybe you can work that out with your lawyer."

Vasquez stood, yawned and then stretched. "But honestly kid, it's looking like whatever happened that day is gonna have you rotting in here the rest of your life. Let's go Blackwell."

Pop's mouth instantly became dry. *She's dead,* he thought as he fought for his water barricades to stay up. His eyes began to burn as tears threatened to fall. *Where the fuck is this C.O.? I need to get out of this room!* The walls began to close in on Pop. *What the fuck did I do?* His thoughts drifted off into his locked down memories.

All the tragedy that Pop encountered in his life he had locked away in a dungeon in his mind. If all those memories were on the forefront the guilt alone would chip away at him. The guard came into the room and cuffed Pop so that they could make their journey back to his cell.

"Miller, I'll reach out again. I'll give you some time to think about all of this," Vasquez said as he followed behind his partner. Their dress shoes echoed against the concrete floors as they made their exit.

The walk back to his cell was unlike the walk towards the interrogation room. Pop heard nothing; all the other inmates and guards screaming around him sounded like nothing more than muffled whispers.

Asia's face appeared in his thoughts, her smile and her eyes. Pop knew he had an unforgiving temper. He'd been that way since a child. He was already beating himself up daily for how things escalated between him and Asia that day. Now that she was gone, it was no more beating himself up. He felt as if he couldn't breathe; after all, she was the air in his lungs.

"Turn around Miller." The guard took the handcuffs off Pop's wrist and left him alone in his cell to just think.

Pop was silently grateful that he hadn't gotten a roommate just yet. He sat on his bunk and let his tears flow without restrictions. He quietly whimpered like a child. His whole world around him was heavily flawed. He had no parents; his father ran out before the ink could even dry on his birth certificate and his mother died when he was thirteen from a crack overdose. That's when Ty found him, showed him the ropes, clothed him, and raised him.

The only family he had besides Ty and the crew was Asia.

"Baby nooo," Pop cried as his snot covered upper quivering lip. He found himself asking this question on more than enough occasions. "What the fuck did I do?" he said lowly as his mind drifted back to that day…

Pop just spent his last four days moving weight out in Maryland. He was supposed to spend seven days out of town, but he moved their entire product in almost half the time. He pushed the pedal to the metal moving at 90 mph down I-95. He was about to turn this four-hour drive into two. Once Pop saw signs for New Jersey, he knew that he was just a few moments from home. This early Sunday morning there was no traffic.

His New Jersey location quickly turned into Manhattan and then Downtown, Brooklyn. The only thing on his mind was getting upstairs to surprise his woman on his early arrival. Ain't never no fucking parks on this block, he thought as he circled his block for a fourth time.

"Damn, where the fuck is my phone?" he said out loud as he dug into the passenger side seat.

After his last drop off in Maryland, he hopped straight on the interstate. He hadn't even checked his phone yet. When he finally dug his phone out of the depths of the leather seat, he saw that he had several missed calls from Ty and Bleek with only one voicemail from Ty.

"Shorty couldn't call one time to check on a niggah," he said as he checked his missed calls.

He was expecting at least one missed call from Asia.

He played back his voicemail.

"Yo, Pop call me when you get this. It's urgent."

The urgency in Ty's voice rattled Pop's core. It was about eight in the morning and he knew that his mentor would be up; he rarely slept in. He placed three calls to Ty but there was no response. Seeing that Bleek called his phone too, he figured that Bleek knew the urgent news as well.

He called Bleek's phone and got an answer on the first ring.

"What's up boy boy?" Bleek said as he inhaled his toxin of choice, marijuana.

"I can't call it but yo, I can't reach Ty and you called me too. What's up?"

Bleek wasn't as close to Pop as Ty but he felt as if he could better tell the youngin' the unfortunate news about his lady.

Ty was something like a father figure for Pop. Bleek knew that if Ty had to share the news it would hurt him as well. He took a deep breath and then just gave it to him straight.

"Asia's been doing coke since Ty's birthday party."

Pop chuckled. "Come on bro, really?" he asked jokingly.

His mind began to go into overdrive as he walked towards his building. Everything else Bleek was saying on the other line was going in one ear and out the other. Her recent behavior that was previously overlooked started to all make sense. She slept all day, her moods were erratic, one day she was happy and then the next she was snappy as hell. And to top it off, she had developed nosebleeds within the past few months.

"Just bro, don't lose your cool. You have to be smart, you have to—"

"Let me call you back," Pop cut off Bleek and then hung up on him as he opened the front door to the apartment that he shared with Asia.

The moment his feet entered the apartment and stepped over the threshold, the stench of marijuana invaded his nostrils. Magazines covered the coffee table and the floor beneath it. The sunrays that peaked through the blinds illuminated the space surrounding him. This place is a fucking mess, he thought to himself.

"Asia!" he yelled as he stormed towards the back of the house. Sniffling could be heard from their bedroom in the back. These niggahs got to be wrong, he thought as he allowed his Timberland boots to carry him to his destination. When he opened the bedroom door, Asia sat idly on her side of the bed with her back facing him.

Her sniffles could be heard.

"What are you crying for?"

Her entire body jumped at the sound of his voice. What is he doing home? she thought as she sprang up off the bed and stood to face him. As soon as she turned around, Pop could see that what Bleek had told him was true. There was a redness that outlined her eyes. Her pupils were glossy and dilated.

A dash of white powder sat gently on the tip of her pointy nose. The black nightstand had ashy white lines of coke residue. Pop stormed in Asia's direction.

"It's not what it looks like," she yelled before her neck was grabbed firmly.

Being this close to her only incensed him more. These signs that he used to ignore all pointed to her using.

"Bitch! Do you know how embarrassing this is?" he screamed.

She punched and clawed at his neck. Tiny trickles of blood danced down his thick neck as she peeled his skin. Asia started to see black spots around the dimly lit room. Oh no, he's killing me, she thought. His grip didn't seem to be loosening. With all her remaining strength she kneed Pop hard in his groin. Instantly, he removed his hand from around her throat to grab his throbbing sack.

Asia ran towards the living room.

"I have to get out of here," she said as she made her way towards the front door.

She was frozen in her tracks when her hand touched the doorknob. She thought about the bags of dope she had on the living room coffee table. She turned around quickly and tossed all the magazines from the surface.

"One, two, three," she counted as she picked up every singular bag.

"You a stupid bitch! You a fucking junkie!" Pop shouted as he grabbed a handful of her hair and wrapped it around his fingers.

"Owww you're hurting me! Get the fuck off me," she squawked.

Her desperate cries fell on deaf ears with Pop, but the neighbors heard her loud and clear.

"This is what the fuck you wanted to ruin everything for! EVERYTHING!" He moved her head closer to the coffee table to put her nose to nose with her powdered white love. *This niggah always warned me of this shit. He always said that this game could change the people around me. He always said to make sure that the ones I love always kept their nose clean.* Pop could hear Ty's chastising in his head.

Growing up, Ty constantly drilled in Pop's head how dangerous their line of work could be to those around them.

"Just let me go! Just let me go!"

Asia's tears poured onto the glass surface. *She deadass not even worth this dumb shit,* Pop thought as his grip loosened.

"Just let me take my stuff and go." Asia began to reach again for the small bags of drugs on the table.

"YOUR STUFF? Bitch, this is my shit! Let me treat you like the thief you are."

Pop banged her head onto the glass table. Tiny shards of glass scattered everywhere. Asia's cries stopped as she laid slumped into the frame of the table. "Now you can get the fuck out!" Pop said as he stood above her body.

"Asia?"

He received no response.

"Yo." He nudged her lower back with the tip of his boot.

Silence filled the messy apartment and fear began to creep into Pop's bones.

"Asia?" he whispered again.

KNOCK KNOCK KNOCK!

"Police, open up!"

Present Day...

Pop couldn't cope with the pain that his mind was putting him through. *I can't do this shit,* he thought as he wiped the tears and snot from his face.

Chapter 16

Toya stood in the mirror and just gazed at her reflection. Her makeup was beat to perfection. Her arched eyebrows dipped in sorrow. She had to ready herself to bury her friend today. Her black Donna Karan dress hugged her curves to a tee. She held onto the vanity's tabletop for support and took a deep breath.

Her life seemed as if it was taking a turn for the worst. Tears slowly walked down her pudgy cheeks. She officially had no one to lean on. Her closest friend would soon be in the grave and Ty was missing in action. A few days prior, Ty had received a call from Riker's Island. Pop was found dead in his cell with both of his wrists slit.

Toya stood by and watched Ty go through his motions. She secretly was happy about Pop's demise; after all, he was the one who murdered her friend. Toya couldn't tell if Ty stayed away because he didn't want to show her that he was hurting or because he blamed her for everything. Whatever the reason, she felt like they needed each other more now than ever.

Toya finally was able to pull herself together. She put on her black fur coat, grabbed her purse and made her way towards the front door.

As soon as she opened the door there Ty was standing on the other side. He looked a mess. His curly fro needed to be trimmed badly. His normal neat appearance seemed to vanish; he looked as if he had lost his way. Toya was grateful that she had on her sunglasses. Her eyes immediately began to water. She wanted to be there for Ty so bad, but she was also hurting, she just didn't know how to fix things. He brushed past her without uttering a word. *How can I fix this?* she thought as a tear slipped from her right eye.

She closed the apartment's door behind her and slowly walked towards the elevators. She wanted desperately to just turn around, walk over the threshold of their home and make things right, but she couldn't. Her feet pushed forward with leaving while her heart was screaming for her to turn around.

When her body was about to follow her heart's request, she thought of how Ty had just breezed past her, his mood so unbothered and detached. In her time of hurt and pain she thought of him, but she felt like he didn't care that she too was hurting. *He doesn't give a fuck,* she thought as she stepped into the elevator. Outside, the chill from the late November air stung her face and quickly dried the trail of her tears, turning them into icicles on her face.

$$$

Ty sat motionless on his sofa. Too much was happening around him too fast for his mind to grasp. His personal life seemed to be crumbling at his feet. The only thing in his life right now that was thriving and afloat was his business in these streets and his money. His inner thoughts began to invade his mind and consume him. The buzzing vibration from his cell phone caught his attention.

Tori: "Hey friend lol… I heard what happened. I'm sorry for your loss. Hope all is well with you, hit me if you feel like it, I'm here for you. Keep your head up, okay?"

Ty eyed the text message that he had just received and smiled. She was still sarcastic. He hadn't smiled at all since he put his little homie in the dirt. *Damn, it's been a while since I heard from her.*

The season had turned over and become anew and here she was reaching out to him. The last time that he saw her quickly played in his mind. He didn't know if it was the weirdly warm October weather that made him take a liking to her or if she genuinely had a spark that caught his eye. Whatever the reason, his curiosity yearned to know more about her.

Ty looked at the cable box to read the time; it was 10:11 a.m. *Would this be a good time to call?*

Well she did just text first, fuck it. Ty shrugged off his doubts as he placed the call. The ringing in his ear caused knots to form in his stomach. So unfamiliar. He didn't know what this feeling was, but he wasn't going to hang up.

"Hello?" Her voice was groggy as if she just had opened her eyes but still to Ty's ears, it was the sweetest sound.

"Hey friend," Ty said coolly, taking a move out of her playbook.

She chuckled slightly at his sarcasm then suddenly her demeanor became more serious.

"Are you okay?" her tone was laced in sorrow; she really cared.

"I'm alright, this happens yo. Thanks for asking."

Ty stretched out on his couch and kicked off his sneakers so that he could put his feet up.

The couple stayed on the phone for about four hours laughing and reminiscing about their different childhoods. Two different worlds that shared the same struggle.

"Na, Ma no lie—" Ty paused his statement to yawn. "Shitttt," he said at the end of his yawn.

"Go to bed Ty," she said softly as she yawned also. "I'm not even tired Ma you—" A yawn escaped his mouth and interrupted him again.

"Boy your yawning is making me yawn." She giggled as she covered her mouth.

"Aight I'm out," he said as he lifted his body from the sofa.

He slowly dragged his feet across the soft carpet towards the bedroom.

"Thanks for the talk Tori," he said appreciatively as he slowly undressed to crawl into his bed.

"Anytime," she responded just before ending the call. Ty pulled the covers over his shoulder and then slowly drifted into a slumber.

$$$

Toya's heart was heavy as she walked into the apartment. She was depressed at how her life was turning out. She walked slowly towards the bedroom and tripped.

"Shit," she mumbled lowly as she kicked Ty's sneakers out of her way.

She missed her friend Asia dearly, but she was somewhat relieved that she was now free of her demons and in a better place.

Once she reached her bedroom's door, she just stared at a sleeping Ty. He was laid flat on his back with his arms stretched across the California king-sized bed. Toya zipped down her dress and then stepped out of it. She needed a moment for her mind to just shut down. Sleep wasn't what her body craved because even then nightmares stomped around in her head. She wanted peace. She wanted to wave the white flag to surrender to Ty. To end this silent war that they had been on. To restore their relationship back to a blissful place.

She crawled into the bed wearing only her black lace panty and bra. She needed Ty's warm touch, so she cuddled up beneath him. She inhaled deeply as his toxic scent invaded her nostrils. Instantly, she had become moist between the legs. Her head rested gently on top of his firm chest. She listened to his heartbeat in her ear.

Boom, boom… boom, boom

Each beat caused her clit to match its rhythm. It had been a while since her and Ty were intimate. She was used to getting her rocks off often, so this drought was unfamiliar to her.

She kissed his chest gently and then began to move slowly down his abdomen. Once she reached his waist, she noticed that his soldier was standing at attention. *You missed me huh?* she thought as she reached into his boxers to free his private area.

She grabbed a hold of his shaft and gently massaged the base.

"Mmmm," he hummed; still his eyes were closed.

Toya placed the head of his dick onto her lips and blew warm air just before she placed the head into her mouth. She sucked on it gently but still firmly.

"Oh shit," Ty mumbled groggily as he clenched his toes tightly together.

His eyes were still closed. Toya grabbed his balls and then massaged lightly as she bobbed her head up and down onto his shaft.

Ty reached down and grabbed a hold of her hair. He guided her as he talked his shit.

"Yea, suck Daddy dick," he said lowly as he licked his lips.

This enticed Toya more; she had begun to pick up her pace.

"Ohhh shittt, Tor—" Ty cut himself short.

He let go of Toya's hair as his eyes opened. There she was, his fiancée, giving him the best blowjob he had ever gotten in his life.

Ty's heart began to race rapidly, not because he was about to climax but because he was about to call out another woman's name. The same woman who taught him what love is was about to be called something other than the name given to her. He watched Toya as she performed at her best.

She was so in tune with his needs. She moaned quietly as she sucked his dick. To Ty, the head felt better before he opened his eyes. A pot of hatred was slowly beginning to simmer in his heart for her. He firmly grabbed Toya's hair and moved her off his shaft.

"Get on your knees, on the bed, all fours," he said flatly as he began to sit up in the bed.

Toya took off her panties and bra and then did exactly what she was told. Her mahogany skin glistened under the sunrays that peeked through their blinds. The arch in her back deepened when she dipped her chest closer towards the mattress. Ty grabbed her waist and then eased into her wetness.

"Sssss, ahhh," she moaned softly as he entered.

Once he was in, he gave forceful thrusts. His balls smacked the back of her hard.

"Owwwww Daddyyy," she moaned.

She didn't remember their lovemaking being this rough. She always enjoyed how gentle Ty was with her. The only thing she could think about as she bit the sheets to keep herself from screaming was how aggressively she was being handled.

He took all his built up rage out on the body in front of him. He was starting to hate Toya because she lied. Maybe with her honestly would have come different outcomes for both Asia and Pop. All this rage clouded around him, so he closed his eyes as he shoved his entire dick into Toya's opening. His mind painted a beautiful picture for him.

He could see Tori in front of him instead with her ass in the air. Her light skin felt soft, her brown hair was wild, and her moan was bringing him to his climax. He pounded harder and more ferociously as he became closer and closer to his climax. In his mind, Tori's moans escaped her lips in pleasure.

He reached down and grabbed a handful of her hair as he continued his strokes.

"Yeaaa Ma! Yeaaaa," he yelled loudly as he pumped in and out.

"Ahhh Daddy, you're hurting me Owwww."

Ty let his seeds spill into her right before he was interrupted from his daydream. When he heard Toya's voice in the back of his mind, he came to. He opened his eyes and looked down to see that Toya had begun to run from him.

Her once arched back was now hunched over like a turtle's shell. She looked back at him and he could see that tears were streaming down her face. The palms of her hands looked white and pale from grabbing the comforter so tight. Immediately, Ty withdrew from her and then laid with his back on the bed.

He could tell that he had really hurt her because moments after he pulled out, she was still in the same position. He didn't know what to do so he had left her there. The normal Ty would have consoled her, would have checked on her, but he wasn't that. He wasn't his normal self.

He stared at the ceiling as he let his thoughts roam. *What the fuck is good with me?* He stood from the bed and then walked into their master bathroom. He ran a bath for her, making sure to add in her favorite Bath and Body Works along with some soothing oils and bath salts. When he went back into the bedroom, he saw that she now sat on the edge of the bed with her head in her hands.

Her wild hair covered her face. He heard her sniffles and then he thought back to the skeleton named Lance that she shoved into her closet all those years ago. He couldn't even imagine how she felt; instantly, he felt like shit.

"I'm sorry Ma," he whispered.

He walked towards her and scooped her into his arms. Once her head rested comfortably onto his chest she cried loudly as he carried her to the bathroom. He placed her into the warm water and then sat on the toilet seat nearby.

She sat in the jetted tub with her knees in her chest. The intimate aspect of their love life was fading quickly; she could sense it. She couldn't stop the tears from flowing so she didn't even try. Ty stared at the light gray wall in front of him as he beat himself up. *I can't keep doing this and treating her like this,* he thought as he looked over to see Toya slowly washing her body in the tub. He reached over to help her wash but when her body flinched with fear, he felt like shit.

He stood from the toilet's top and then walked out of the bathroom. His eyes had begun to water. He would have never in a million years thought he would ever feel what he was feeling right now at this moment. *I don't love her how I used to.* His thoughts rattled his core as he took a seat on the edge of the bed.

Chapter 17

One month later…

Ty sat back in his seat as always at meetings, lost in his thoughts. He twirled his pinky ring as he listened to Bleek talk. As he looked around at the table of men, emptiness washed over him. He was two soldiers short. Dro was late, which was unusual, and Pop was in the heavens now. *His ass probably running hell with two bad bitches at his side and a bottle of Henny in his hand,* Ty thought as he smiled.

"Yo, sorry mi late," Dro said quickly as he rushed towards his empty seat.

Sweat covered his forehead as he walked swiftly. Ty looked at him, giving him a head nod to accept his apology.

"Yo Dro, we can fill you in later. We damn near done here," Bleek said as he continued, "Is it anything you want to say?" he asked Ty as he turned in his direction. Ty breathed deeply before he spoke. This was their first meeting since Pop's suicide and it just didn't feel right. "I want all of y'all to continue to do what you're doing but some changes are soon approaching. The connect is retiring and—" Rex, one of the bosses at the table, cut Ty off.

"So, wait what… we about to be in a drought or some shit?"

Everyone at the table except for Bleek's curiosity wandered. Bleek already knew what was soon to come. He was always the first to know what was up because he was second in command.

"If you will let me finish, I can get there," Ty said before he breathed deeply and then continued, "There will be no drought. As you all know, the connect was my father's right-hand man. He's my godfather. He's old now so he's stepping down. He has no children, so he wants me to step up. My trip to DR next month will finalize things. By taking his spot, I will be stepping down from the team, but I think Bleek can fill my shoes."

He looked to his right-hand man and then gently applied pressure to his shoulder.

Rex smiled widely. "So this means we're about to get some more paper."

Everyone around the table took in the information and was thrilled. Bleek stood from his chair as Ty sat back down.

"Effective next month, when I step up, I have to choose a right hand. Someone who will be to me what I am to Ty, trustworthy and loyal. My right hand will be Dro. That's cool with you, bro?" Bleek asked as he stared the dark-skinned man in the eye.

"Let's get di paper brudda," Dro said as he wiped the sweat from his forehead and smiled brightly.

"Dro come turn up with me and Ty," Bleek said eagerly.

"Mi can't man. I got something to handle," Dro quickly declined.

"Alright y'all, let's get the fuck outta here," Ty said as he rose from his seat and began to put on his Moncler coat.

The group of now eight all walked out of the warehouse and into the snowy December night. Luxury cars all parked on an angle in front of the warehouse. "Same date next month," Ty called out to the scattered men. Dro walked hurriedly to his car, got in and peeled away quickly.

"It doesn't make any sense to still go out if the niggah not going. He just got the biggest promotion ever and he ain't want to celebrate. Fuck is up with him?" Ty asked Bleek as they walked to their cars that were parked side by side.

Bleek zipped his coat up to his neck. *He is moving kind of funny,* he thought as he kicked his feet on the side of his car to remove the snow from them before he got in.

"I'm gone see what's up with that," he said reassuringly.

Ty got into his car and rolled down the window so that the two men could continue to talk from both cars.

"Yo, Eternity coming over to my crib and shit. Her ass wants to put up a tree for tomorrow. I know it's Christmas and shit but if you still going through it at home, come over," Bleek said.

Ty's facial expression turned to distress almost instantly. He didn't have to tell Bleek that he was still going through it because the lines that creased in his forehead told the story when he asked.

"Aight bro," he said as he reversed his car from the curb.

It had been an entire month and him and Toya still had not gotten back on track. They slept under the same roof, but they hardly ever spoke. He would wake up in the morning, shower and be out the door before her eyes even opened. He treaded lightly around her because he had yet to find the words to let her know how he was feeling lately.

It was obvious that their feelings for one another had changed drastically, but it seemed as if neither one of them wanted to say it out loud. Bonds like the one that they once shared were never supposed to be broken, cracked or damaged, sure, but never broken.

$$$

Ty pulled into his parking garage, cut his engine and just sat inside of the car. It was nine at night; for them it was early. So, he knew that Toya would be sashaying around the house with her wine glass in one hand and the remote to the stereo system in the other. He smiled as he thought about how well he knew her. He closed his eyes and pictured how she would sing to old school songs and sway her hips to the rhythm of whatever beat was playing.

Toya's face soon faded in his mind and was replaced with Tori. He recalled the day he had first met her and how she sang along with the music that was playing. Over the past couple of weeks, Ty and

Tori had been talking more, phone calls and text. He kept his distance from her because he honestly didn't trust himself around her. The last thing he wanted was to kick down a door with Tori when he still hadn't closed one with Toya. *I can't do this shit no more,* he thought as he rubbed his hands over his face repeatedly.

There was no way that he was going to Bleek's house without handling his business first. He knew if Eternity was going to be there so would Tori. *I must let her go.* He locked his car doors behind him and made his way towards the elevators. Once he stepped off the elevator, as predicted, he heard music playing from down the hall. He unlocked and opened the door to find Toya sitting on the couch Indian style eating popcorn and listening to music.

Instead of one of her silk kimono robes, she wore a plush cotton bathrobe. Ty could tell that she had just gotten out of the shower by how damp her hair looked. Silky strands fell from her bun and stuck to her forehead. She turned down the music and then looked his way.

"Hey," she said flatly.

"What's up," he mumbled as he took off his Timberland boots at the door. He sat on the couch beside her and exhaled deeply.

"What's wrong with you?" she asked as she chewed her popcorn daintily.

Her pink-colored nails dug deep into the bowl to retrieve more popcorn. Ty remained silent. He hadn't yet decided how to say this. He looked over at Toya and took in her beauty.

Her legs were oiled down. She always moisturized her skin as soon as she stepped out of the shower. Her robe cut low in the front, exposing her bust line. He looked deep into her green eyes and noticed how flushed her cheeks looked. She was glowing so this made it harder for him.

She wiped a popcorn kernel from the side of her mouth before she spoke.

"I said what's wrong?"

She turned her body to face him.

"Ma, this isn't working," he said quickly.

Toya's chest grew heavy; she knew exactly where he was going with this.

"What exactly isn't working?"

Her voice cracked as she spoke. Ty rubbed his face once over, then he placed his face into his hands as he spoke.

"This Ma, us…"

Toya's tears fell freely. These words were some that she thought she would never hear. Ever since the situation with Asia, the two had never gotten the chance to get back on track. It seemed like there was never a time to mend what was quickly cracking. She thought of everything but a split. This was something that she thought would never be.

"Don't cry Ma," he said as his own eyes began to water.

His heart was beginning to break. This was throwing away almost eight years. Suddenly, Toya felt sick to her stomach, so she ran to the bathroom.

As soon as she stepped over the threshold, she dived head first for the toilet. She couldn't stop the contents of her stomach from coming up.

Ty ran after her and stood at the bathroom door as he watched her cry and vomit. He walked over to her to try and console her.

"Please, baby girl—" He rubbed her back gently.

"Don't touch me Tyshawn!" she interrupted as she cried and held onto the toilet's sides for dear life.

Ty withdrew his hand from her back and rubbed the sides of his face instead. Tears slid down his cheeks involuntarily. This moment right here was why he was trying his hardest to postpone this conversation. How could a perfect love go so wrong? His mind couldn't grasp it, but he couldn't ignore the voice screaming in his head anymore. Something had changed between them and he needed space to breathe.

Toya stood in front of the double sink to wash her face and hands. She looked at her own reflection in the mirror. Her eyes had a tint of red from her tears; as always when she cried her eyes instantly became puffy. The throw up feeling she felt came again, she rubbed her stomach to try and soothe her nausea. She stared blankly at her reflection and cried harder.

Ty stood nearby and just watched as she went from calm to a crying mess. *Why now God?* she asked herself as she cried. The feeling of her having to throw up just wouldn't subside. She quickly remembered that earlier that day she had taken a pregnancy test since her menstrual was five days late. Her cycle was never late and as expected, the test was positive.

She didn't even get the chance to tell Ty the news. *I'm damn sure not saying anything now, before he thinks that I'm tryna keep him here. If he wants to leave, he can get the fuck on!*

She closed her eyes as she grabbed hold of the sink surface. She needed to brace herself for the question she was about to ask.

"Is there someone else?"

The question threw Ty completely off guard. He rushed to her side and wrapped his arms around her from behind.

"No Ma, never," he lied as he kissed the sides of her face gently.

His hands interlocked over her stomach which caused her to break down. *Why God? Why did he have to put his hands there?* Toya felt like the air was leaving her lungs. To say that she was heartbroken would be an understatement. Besides losing a lover, she was losing her very best friend.

"So then why are you leaving me?" she cried hysterically. She'd felt the rift between them, but she held on.

Ty turned her to face him. He wiped her tears and she had begun to wipe his. They were both broken. Walking away from one another was killing them but they both knew that deep down inside if they both stayed, they would start to resent and hate one another.

"Look me in my eyes right now Toya. If you can tell me honestly, and I mean honestly baby that you are happy here with me, then I will take back everything that I just said. I will stay baby and we will work this out just me and you. We can give this another shot."

Toya breathed in and out quickly as she cried. "I... I..." She had begun to talk but tears took over.

She couldn't say it to him. He was right, she was indeed unhappy and had been for some time. Realistically, even if she did tell him that she wanted him to stay she knew that it would only be postponing the inevitable. He hugged her tightly and she cried gently on his chest.

"I can't do this without you Ty."

He stroked her hair as he held her.

"Yes, you can Ma." He kissed her forehead repeatedly. "You're strong baby girl. I saw you survive shit that others can't, and I'll always be here. You will never have to worry about money. Do you hear me?"

He lifted her chin so that she could look him in his eyes. She stared deep into his brown eyes only to cry harder. Here he was thinking that she was saying she couldn't survive living without him; that she knew she could do. She felt like she couldn't be a new mom without him with her. She backed away from his embrace and wiped her tears away.

She stared down at her left hand and slowly began to take off her engagement ring.

"Toya, I swear to God you better not give that ring back," Ty's voice was firm.

Just as she controlled her tears, they came flooding again.

"You don't want me Tyshawn, so what the fuck am I keeping this for?" she screamed.

Ty pinched the bridge of his nose to control himself. It wasn't that he didn't want her; he just wanted to break away before any more damage could be done to them.

He felt like he had already lost his lover; he didn't want to lose his friend next.

"Word to my father, Latoya, if you take that ring off your finger, I'm gonna lose my cool. I'm tryna save us. I don't love you any less! And that's on my life. I don't care if you or I move on, NO female can ever get the piece of me that you have."

Toya stopped removing the ring from her finger and just leaned up against the sink. They stared in each other's eyes and Toya thought maybe, just maybe that she should tell him about her recently discovered pregnancy.

"Is this really what you want to do? You want us to be done?" she asked lowly.

Her gaze never shifted from his.

"I want you to be happy. I want to be happy Ma," he said dejectedly.

"Okay," she said flatly as she wiped her face.

She walked out of the bathroom and into the bedroom; she needed to be alone. She laid in the bed under the covers in a fetal position. Here was when she made it up in her mind that she couldn't say anything about her being pregnant, at least not right now. For one, she didn't want the pity stay and secondly, she didn't want to stand in the way of his happiness. She was true to Mase's lyrics: I want to see you happy even if it's not with me.

After several moments Ty left the bathroom as well. He walked past Toya and headed straight for the front door to exit. It was midnight, Christmas Day, and his heart was shattered into a million pieces.

"I need a fucking drink," he mumbled to himself as he walked to his car. All the bars near him were starting to close for the holiday. Late night on holidays in New York equaled gunplay so most of the businesses shut down early.

The next best thing to a bar that Ty knew of was Bleek's house. He had bottles shelved for days over there. Ty had intentions on indulging in every drink that his brother's house had to offer.

"What up boy boy?" Bleek answered his phone as he filled his lungs with smoke.

"I'm coming uptown, so you better be up niggah," Ty said as he pulled out of the parking garage.

"Yea I'm up. We in here smoking," he responded.

"We?"

"Yea Me, E and Tori."

"I'm on my way."

Ty hung up the phone and then made his way towards the Brooklyn Bridge. His tires splashed through the snow as he made his way to the Bronx. He knew it was fucked up, but he was yearning to be around Tori. He had to know if the feelings he was starting to develop for her were true…

C. Wilson

THE END

A look into:
Love in between the White Lines
Part 2

Chapter 1

The sunrays that peeked through the blinds woke Toya from her sleep. It was Christmas morning and the space beside her went undisturbed. *So, he didn't come home last night?* she thought as she searched the house for her cellphone. The apartment she and Ty shared bore no Christmas tree or decorations. The residents of this space weren't in the holiday spirit and it showed. She slowly dragged her feet across the soft carpet. Tears involuntarily fell from her eyes as she walked towards the living room. She needed to find her phone. She had to speak to someone, anyone that could take her mind off the heartbreak that ached in her chest. She sat gently on her leather sofa and sighed deeply as she skimmed through her contacts. She found just who she thought she could pour her sorrows into. She didn't need to be judged and she didn't need to hear negativity from anyone.

The phone rung for a while in her ear while her stomach did somersaults. She didn't know if these were signs from her baby telling her to eat or if they were nervous butterflies.

"Hello?" a woman said on the other end of the receiver.

Toya sat quietly as she listened to the woman's voice. It was just like she remembered.

"Hello?" the woman said once more, this time with more attitude.

Toya's voice broke as she spoke, "Auntie Ke, I need you."

$$$

Six whole days had passed since Ty had left home. He hadn't received any calls from Toya, and he didn't even try calling her. He didn't go back home because honestly, he felt as if he couldn't face her. *What the fuck did I get myself into?* he thought as he stared fixedly at the head of the beauty that was fast asleep on his chest. His fingers twirled in Tori's locks as his mind wandered. He couldn't seem to get Toya's face out of his mind. The night he had left home replayed in his head constantly. Although the cause of her tears was of his doing, he looked past her stained cheeks and noticed just how beautiful she was. She looked radiant and her skin glowed as he figuratively snatched her heart from her chest. Tori yawned, breaking him from his daydream…

COMING SOON

C. Wilson

Follow C. Wilson on social media

Instagram: @authorcwilson

Facebook: @CelesteWilson

Join my reading group on Facebook: Cecret Discussionz

Twitter: @Authorcwilson_

***

Love In Between The White Lines

Tell me what you think of this story in a customer review.

Thank you,

Xoxo C. Wilson

C. Wilson

Available on Amazon

CPSIA information can be obtained
at www.ICGtesting.com
Printed in the USA
LVHW091517011119
636084LV00001B/80/P